Now
Ha...
ro...
by An...
com...
on the movie screen

starring
KEIR DULLEA · SUSAN PENHALIGON

Leopard in the Snow

Guest Stars
KENNETH MORE · BILLIE WHITELAW

featuring GORDON THOMSON as MICHAEL
and **JEREMY KEMP** as **BOLT**

Produced by JOHN QUESTED and CHRIS HARROP
Screenplay by ANNE MATHER and JILL HYEM
Directed by GERRY O'HARA
An Anglo-Canadian Co-Production

WELCOME
TO THE WONDERFUL WORLD
OF *Harlequin Romances*

Interesting, informative and entertaining,
each Harlequin Romance portrays an appealing
and original love story. With a varied array
of settings, we may lure you on an African safari,
to a quaint Welsh village, or an exotic riviera
location—anywhere and everywhere that adventurous
men and women fall in love.

As publishers of Harlequin Romances, we're
extremely proud of our books. Since 1949,
Harlequin Enterprises has built its publishing
reputation on the solid base of quality and
originality. Our stories are the most popular
paperback romances sold in North America; every
month, eight new titles are released and sold at
nearly every book-selling store in Canada and the
United States.

A free catalogue listing all available Harlequin Romances
can be yours by writing to the

HARLEQUIN READER SERVICE,
(In the U.S.) M.P.O. Box 707, Niagara Falls, N.Y. 14302
(In Canada) Stratford, Ontario, Canada N5A 6W2

or use order coupon at back of book.

We sincerely hope you enjoy reading
this Harlequin Romance.

Yours truly,

THE PUBLISHERS

Harlequin Romances

Island
Masquerade

by

SALLY WENTWORTH

Harlequin Books

TORONTO • LONDON • NEW YORK • AMSTERDAM • SYDNEY

Original hardcover edition published in 1977
by Mills & Boon Limited

ISBN 0-373-02155-0

Harlequin edition published April 1978

PRINTED IN U.S.A.

CHAPTER ONE

FAR below them Felicity could see the dark shadow of the plane, like a small bird sliding and dipping in the sun over the undulating waves of the ocean. Soon, she knew, the moment that she both longed for and dreaded would arrive, but there was still a little time to compose herself before the first of the chain of islands came into view, and before the plane landed at Trenaka, the largest island in the group, and the only one that boasted a runway and a few buildings that bore the pretentious title of 'Airport'.

Up here, in the cabin of the local aeroplane with many of the native West Indian passengers in their brightly coloured clothes, laughing and chattering happily among themselves, it was hard to remember that less than twenty-four hours ago she had been standing on the windswept platform of a station in a small town on the south coast of England saying goodbye to her mother. The sun had not been shining then; it had been raining, with that fine drizzling rain that isn't worth putting an umbrella up for, but which makes you feel damp and miserable through to your bones.

There had been no tears at their parting. Rather her mother had been happy to see her go, her eyes unnaturally bright as she gloated over the extraordinary stroke of luck which had befallen them. Mrs Lambert took hold of her daughter's hands and pressed them tightly in hers, not from affection, but to better convey the urgency of her words.

'It's fate, I'm sure it is. That you should have been accepted for the post of assistant doctor, and then to find out that *he*'s there—the man who caused your poor brother's death. He's no better than a murderer, worse even, because he got away scot free. But when I wrote to Cousin Elspeth telling her that you were going to work on Trenaka and she replied that Bruce Gresham was there—well, I just knew that it was meant!'

She held Felicity's hands even tighter and stared into her eyes intently. 'Promise me, Felicity, that if you can find a way to punish him for what he did you'll take it.'

'Oh, Mother, please!' Felicity had protested, but she had known it was no use. Ever since her brother's death ten years ago her mother had been filled with hatred against the man who had caused it.

'You were such a child, it wasn't the same for you, but for me . . .' Mrs Lambert closed her eyes and Felicity saw the lines of pain and sorrow etched deep into her mother's face. 'Please, dear, please do this for me.'

Felicity felt her own heart fill with hatred for the man who had caused such unhappiness. Returning the pressure of her mother's hands, she said, 'All right, Mother. If I can find a way, any way at all, then I'll make him pay for what he did.'

Then, mercifully, the train had drawn noisily into the station and there had been time for nothing more except a hurried peck on the cheek given to her almost as an after-thought when Felicity had impulsively hugged the tall, gaunt-faced woman who was all she had in the world.

The islands were in sight now, their long palm-fringed beaches of golden-white coral sand giving way to rich green interiors with white-painted houses and bungalows clustered in the valleys and on the slopes of the hills. The smiling steward was making his way down the plane warn-ing everyone to fasten their seat-belts, and Felicity quickly clicked hers into place. My brother's murderer, she thought; for it had been murder, her mother had said so. The police had said it was an accident when they pulled Peter's body

6

from the tangled wreckage of the Jaguar, but her mother had stopped screaming suddenly and said, 'No. it's murder.'

The plane touched down lightly on the concrete runway. She was in Trenaka. Felicity had sworn to be revenged on Bruce Gresham, her brother's killer, and now fate had brought her here to keep her vow.

As she stepped from the plane the heat seemed to rise towards her and she instantly felt overdressed in the neat grey flannel suit she had chosen to travel in. Hastily she fumbled in her large handbag for her sunglasses; never having been abroad before she found the brilliant hardness of the light almost painful to her eyes. It did not take long to clear the few passengers through Customs and she was just turning away when a burly West Indian swooped on her luggage and quickly festooned himself with her cases.

'Hey, be careful with that!' Felicity exclaimed in alarm as she saw her precious medical bag being placed under his muscular arm.

The big man gave her a grin to match his size. 'Don't you worry, miss, I'll be careful. If you'll come along with me, I'll take you to Doctor Mac.'

Felicity felt slightly taken aback but did as she was asked and followed him into a small reception area.

'You found her all right, then, Joey?' The man who advanced to meet her could not have been any other nationality than a Scot; he was only of average height but had a wiry body with sturdy shoulders, and the once bright ginger of his hair, now edged with grey, gave an indication of his warm smile and firm handshake.

'Welcome to Trenaka, lassie. Did you have a good journey?'

Felicity smiled rather shyly back, liking the look of this man who was to be her boss at the island hospital.

'Away with you, man! You haven't even introduced yourself. I'm Ellen MacAllister, my dear, and this is Ian, my husband, but everyone calls him Mac. The man who carried your cases is our house-boy, Joey. Now I expect you'll be looking forward to a good cup of tea and a shower after that long flight, so we'll be off home to the bungalow right away.'

It was obvious that this rather plump, grey-haired woman with the motherly smile was used to organising, for she soon had them settled in a big American car with the luggage safely stowed in the boot. Felicity sat next to her in the back and was soon completely at ease with this couple with whom she was to make her home. Joey drove them away, along a road bordered with the tender purples and greens of young mango leaves, and everywhere about them hung the rich scent of fermenting fields brown from reaping. There were small houses, gay with lines of washing, and men and women singing as they worked in the fields.

As Felicity greedily drank in all the new sights and listened to the MacAllisters as they pointed out special points of interest to her, she thought that the island seemed to be a very happy place. For one brief agonising moment she longed with all her heart to be just what she appeared to be; a girl who had come to take up a job on this sunny, exotic island in the West Indies. Then she pulled herself together and mentally straightened her shoulders; there could be no happiness for her on Trenaka. Somehow she must do what she had to do and then leave this lovely place behind her for ever.

Soon they were approaching the sea and within a few minutes had arrived at the MacAllisters' bungalow. Like most of the houses she had seen this was painted white and had a long veranda running the length of the seaward side. There was no formal garden, just lawns and a patio shaded by breadfruit trees with a riot of bougainvillaea and oleander acting as a hedge between that and the neighbouring property.

Ellen took her through a large living-room and pointed out the bathroom as she led the way to the room that was to be Felicity's.

'I hope you find the room to your liking,' she said as she

ushered Felicity in. 'It was my daughter's room when she was at home, but she's off and married to an American who came here for a holiday, and she lives in California now.'

Felicity noted a hint of wistfulness in her voice. 'You must miss her very much,' she sympathised.

'Och, well, she's very happy and they try to get here as often as they can. Perhaps when Mac has his next leave we'll maybe go and visit them this time.'

'Do you have any other children, Mrs MacAllister?'

'Aye, I have two sons, both away at the university in Edinburgh,' Ellen answered proudly. 'You'll meet them when they come home for the long vacation.'

They were interrupted by Joey, who came into the room backwards carrying all Felicity's luggage which he carefully set on the floor, his face set in his usual broad grin.

'I do hope he didn't strain himself carrying all my cases,' Felicity remarked. 'He could have brought them in one at a time.'

'Och, you'll find that Joey never does things by halves,' laughed her hostess. 'He's one of the best house-boys in the district.' As Joey must have been at least thirty the description of house-boy seemed somewhat incongruous, but Mrs MacAllister explained that it was just a name for a general servant and that some house-boys on the island were in their seventies!

'I'll leave you now to unpack. Dinner is at eight o'clock. I didn't think you'd want company on your first night, so there are just the three of us, but I've arranged a wee dinner party for tomorrow so that you can meet some of our friends.'

Slowly, knowing that it would take some time to become used to the unaccustomed heat, Felicity started to unpack her cases, carefully hanging her new dresses in the spacious wardrobe and folding the soft, lace-adorned underwear into the matching chest of drawers. She had so much enjoyed the outing to London for the entirely new wardrobe that her mother had insisted she buy for the trip. Luckily her father had left them a comfortable allowance which was more than adequate to keep them in the rambling period house at Alnswick in which Felicity had spent a happy childhood, and which she loved as only a house of childhood memories can be loved.

But all that had ended abruptly ten years ago, after the car crash. The house had been sold and they had moved to the south, to a flat near to Felicity's school, and later, when she had gone to medical college, her mother had moved to be near her, insisting that she come home at night and not allowing her to live in like the other students. So she had always been different, the odd one out who had to go home to Mother every night. Some of the students had made jokes about her, others had pitied her, especially when she had been forbidden to join them socially. Felicity had watched the other girls going out on dates, seen them 'go steady' with their boy-friends and attended many of their weddings. But she had always gone dutifully home to her mother. Only once had she rebelled. There had been a third year student to whom she was attracted and they had gone out to a concert together. When her mother found out she had become hysterical with anger and had suffered a slight stroke; so whenever a young man fell under the spell of her swirling golden hair and dark-lashed amber eyes, she had firmly refused anything more than the friendly camaraderie of a fellow student.

The bathroom was very modern and the shower cool as a mountain stream on her hot skin. Felicity had an idea she would be spending quite a lot of her time under that shower if the heat of today was anything to go by. Having changed into a simple cotton shift dress and repaired her make-up, she joined her hosts on the veranda where they were enjoying a pre-dinner sherry.

'Come and join us, my dear.' Ellen indicated a chair near to hers while the doctor rose to get her a drink. 'It's so nice to have someone young about the house again. We have lots of friends who pop in all the time, of course, but it's not the same. When the bairns are here they have their own friends round whenever they like, and I want you to feel free to do the same when you've been here long enough to get to know people.'

'Thank you, Mrs MacAllister, you're very kind,' Felicity said gratefully.

'Och, it's nothing. And you're to call me Ellen, or Mrs Mac. Everybody does,' the older woman explained comfortably.

'Are there many people about my age on the island?' Felicity managed to make the question sound merely casual, but she awaited the answer with beating heart. Her mother had been told of Bruce Gresham's job in the Civil Service through a distant relation who still lived at Alnswick, but there was always the brain-chilling possibility that he had recently been transferred to another post.

'Living here the whole time, do you mean?' It was the doctor who answered. 'Well, there's my present assistant at the hospital, Geoffrey Lord, who's a few years older than you. You'll meet him tomorrow when I show you round the hospital.'

'Then there are the Marshes,' interrupted his wife. 'Gillian and Colin. Colin works for the Agricultural Department and travels round the islands a good deal, so Gillian will be pleased to have your company for swimming and parties. When you can spare the time, that is,' she added somewhat hastily as she felt her husband's eye upon her.

Their gingham-frocked maid then came to fetch them to dinner and it was a little time before Felicity managed to steer the conversation back to the subject that interested her. 'You said you had invited some friends round for tomorrow evening,' she reminded Ellen. 'Will the people you've told me about be among your guests?'

'Not Geoff, because he'll be on duty at the hospital,' Ellen replied. 'But Gillian and Colin will be coming and also two other youngish couples, the Sinclairs and the Lloyds, and then there's David Cameron, who's in the

11

Ministry of Overseas Development. He's a fine upstanding young man and I ken you'll get along with him fine,' her hostess added hopefully.

Felicity grinned inwardly; it seemed that Ellen wouldn't be above a little harmless matchmaking if she was given half a chance!

'Is there anyone else, or are those all the names I have to try and remember?' she asked with a smile.

'No, we thought that would be enough for one night,' Mac answered with a twinkle in his eye as he looked across at his wife.

'You mean you thought it was enough,' Ellen said with some asperity. 'I could have asked many more. Diane Cunningham, for instance. I seriously considered inviting her because she's the Governor's social secretary and would have been very useful for you to know, but she seems to be escorted everywhere by Bruce lately, and as he's away until next week I decided against asking her.'

'Bruce?' Felicity's voice seemed to stick in her throat as the name she had been waiting all evening to hear was mentioned at last.

'Och, I'm sorry. That's Bruce Gresham. He's in the Foreign Office and is one of the senior administration officers here.'

'Is he engaged to—what did you say her name was—Diane Cunningham?' Felicity's hand hardly shook as she helped herself from a vegetable tureen in front of her.

'No, not yet. Although Bruce is a very ambitious person and he's over young for the position he holds. Diane is a relation of the Governor's wife and could be helpful in furthering his career, so I suppose they will make a match of it eventually, but Bruce doesn't seem in any great hurry.'

'Now then, Ellen, you've been gossiping over-long,' her husband reproved her. 'Felicity will have plenty of time to meet everyone soon enough and will probably be glad when the tourists start arriving so that she can see some new faces.'

12

'Do you have many tourists?' Felicity was glad to change the subject even though she hardly took in Mac's answer. The remainder of the meal seemed to drag on as the doctor talked of the hospital and Ellen of the delights in store for her on the island. As soon as she decently could she pleaded tiredness after her journey and escaped to her room. Felicity could remember nothing of the conversation or recall even the taste of the strange, spiced dishes that she had eaten; all she could think of was Ellen's casual 'he's away until next week'. So she had a little respite, a little time to try and find out as much as she could about her enemy before his return, for only by learning as much as she could about him would she find some weakness that would lead to his downfall.

But how do you go about ruining a man? Felicity wondered. How do you set about destroying a man so utterly that he will never again be able to make anything of his life? Slowly she took the photograph of Peter from the drawer where she had carefully placed it after unpacking. Her mother had insisted that she bring it, although really it was unnecessary, for she knew by heart the handsome young features that smiled back at her so confidently from the frame. He had been twenty-three when he was killed, nearly eight years her senior and the spoilt darling of both Felicity and her mother. Not very like Felicity to look at, Peter had resembled more their dark-haired father who had died when Felicity was very young. Perhaps that was why Mrs Lambert had so preferred Peter to herself, she thought without rancour, for she too had loved and hero-worshipped him with all her heart.

She stood the photograph on the little bedside table and, taking out her writing pad, wrote a hasty letter to her mother to let her know that all was well; that Bruce Gresham was still based on Trenaka. Of secondary importance she added that she had arrived safely. Then she locked the photograph away in the drawer of her desk and slipped wearily into bed. The night seemed to be alive with alien sounds; the constant croaking of frogs in the bushes and the rustling of a light breeze in the orange and lemon trees. These were so different from the noises of people and traffic that Felicity was used to that for a long while she lay awake, but at last exhaustion overcame her and she fell into a troubled, uneasy sleep.

Life on the island started in the cool of the early morning and it seemed hardly any time at all before Betsy, the maid, was knocking on Felicity's door to waken her.

'Good morning, miss. Breakfast will be ready in half an hour.'

Quickly Felicity showered and dressed in a white pleated skirt and print blouse, clipping her hair back from her face in the style she always used when working. She was about to dab some perfume on when she realised it would be superfluous on Trenaka, for already the air was heady with the scents of the flowers from the garden.

Breakfast was an informal meal with Ellen still in her housecoat and Mac reading the local paper while he ate. Felicity chose fresh orange juice and newly-baked crusty rolls.

'Betsy picked the oranges out of the garden this morning and she bakes the bread and rolls herself,' her hostess informed her.

'They smell delicious.'

Ellen smiled indulgently as she watched Felicity bite into another roll. 'Now don't let Mac talk you into overdoing things on your first day. He's so wrapped up in yon hospital of his that he forgets other people aren't used to the climate and expects them to do the same as he does.'

'Now then, Ellen, who's the doctor here, me or you? I'll take good care of the lass. I'm only going to introduce her to the rest of the staff today and take her for a look round the wards so that she can get an idea of the type of ailments we have to cope with. Then I'll bring her back for lunch and a rest and you can show her some of the island

14

this afternoon. But don't think that you can deprive me of my new assistant every day, woman.' He wagged a playful finger at his wife. 'I ken fine you'd like to have her home here with you, to show her off to your friends and to take her shopping with you in Trenaka town.'

Ellen wrinkled her nose at him and went into the kitchen to give some instructions to Betsy, and to Joey who had just arrived, but she was at the door to wave goodbye to them as they set off for the hospital in Mac's car.

'Do you drive, lassie?' Mac enquired as they made their way through the outskirts of the town.

'Yes, I found it necessary to learn while I was in general practice in England.'

'I'm glad to hear it, for you'll find that you need a car to visit the clinics on the other side of the island. I'll put in an application for one for you at the Administration Office, but in the meantime one of the orderlies can drive you wherever you want to go, and Ellen has her own little car for pottering round the island on social visits, which I'm sure she will be pleased to lend you.'

Already the town was thronged with people hurrying to work, and Felicity laughed aloud as she saw an opensided, canvas-topped bus travelling in the opposite direction, absolutely bursting at the seams with baskets, sacks, men, women and children, and what looked to be a coop of terrified hens tied precariously on the back. The name 'Gaiety' was painted in large colourful letters on the front.

'Don't they have numbers?' asked Felicity, turning to watch the bus as it passed them.

'No, nothing so staid. They all have very splendid and dignified names like "Star of the East", or "Western Pride". The one you saw was from the country and was bringing everyone from the outlying villages in to do their shopping and trading at the market.'

'I'd like to take a ride on one,' Felicity exclaimed impulsively.

Dr MacAllister chuckled good-naturedly. 'You'll find it

15

quite an experience, I can tell you. But you probably won't be able to sit down afterwards for some time. They're positive bone-shakers!'

After threading his way skilfully through the traffic and the pedestrians who seemed to consider the road as an extended pavement, the doctor pulled up in front of a long, low building which was the main block of the hospital. Felicity felt a thrill of excitement run through her at the familiar antiseptic smell which enveloped them as they entered. A smiling young woman, her light brown hair cut into a neat pageboy, rose to greet them from a desk in the reception area.

'Good morning, doctor.' Her voice was soft and husky and gave an added charm to her already attractive appearance.

'Morning to you, Edwina. This is our new assistant, Dr Lambert. And this, Felicity, is Edwina Draycott, who is a hive of efficiency and runs the place like clockwise, so don't dare to be a minute late or she'll give you the rough side of her tongue.'

Both girls laughed at Mac's transparent joke and shook hands.

'If there is anything you need or want to know, Dr Lambert, please don't hesitate to ask me. I'm here at the desk all through the day.'

'Thank you, I shall certainly remember that,' Felicity smiled warmly, liking the look of the pretty receptionist.

They left her and went into Mac's office where she found a starched white coat hanging ready for her. Together they set off to cover the wards and soon she was immersed in introductions to nurses and orderlies, case records of illnesses, accidents, births and deaths, the trolley of medicines, the cupboards of instruments and drugs. Felicity had been in general practice for several months before taking this post, but being in a hospital again was like coming home. She felt completely at ease here; it was her world and she loved it.

Mac saw the bright, alert look in her amber eyes, answered her interested, intelligent questions and was satisfied. He had had his doubts when he heard he was to have such a newly qualified doctor as his second assistant, and a slip of a girl at that, but now he was content. She would do.

It was in the women's surgical ward that they encountered Mac's other assistant, Geoffrey Lord, who was just finishing the usual tests on a woman who was to have an operation later that day. He was tall, about thirty-two, and rather flamboyantly handsome, but there were hardening lines around his mouth. He raised a somewhat cynical eyebrow when introduced to Felicity.

'Well, well, things are looking up!' His eyes quite openly appraised her lovely face and slender figure so that Felicity had a hard time to stop herself from blushing under his scrutiny. 'You, my dear doctor, are certainly going to make the residents of Trenaka sit up and take notice, both male and female.'

'Don't take any notice of his blather, lassie,' Mac advised her. 'He just puts on that act to try to give the impression that he's a man of the world; but really he's scared stiff of women. Let's go and see if Edwina can find us a cup of coffee.'

To Felicity's surprise, Geoffrey Lord didn't try to repudiate this but merely leered knowingly at her and followed them back to the office, where they found a coffee tray already awaiting them. The talk was mainly of work and Felicity soon realised that Dr Lord knew his job, and that despite his derogatory attitude, the two men had a complete understanding of each other and made an excellent team. Listening to their conversation, Felicity felt very much the new girl, but Mac made every effort to include her, telling her of their plans and hopes for the future of the hospital.

'We pay regular visits to clinics that we have established on the smaller islands in the group,' he told her. 'I very

17

much hope that eventually you will take over some of these visits and also establish family planning sessions for the native women. We badly need to control the population in this area. It will be quite a challenge, though, as many of the people are still influenced by the ancient religions and voodoos, especially those living on the more remote islands.'

Felicity was immediately interested in his plans and questioned him so eagerly about them that Geoff laughed at her derisively and even Mac threw up his hands in mock dismay.

'There's plenty of time to discuss it, lass, but I have to go over to the wharf and collect some medical supplies this morning, so I'll leave you with Geoff. Ask him all the questions you like; he loves to hear the sound of his own voice.'

After Mac's departure Geoff again assumed his cynical attitude towards her, but Felicity wasn't going to stand for that. 'Look,' she told him firmly, 'you may think that you were put on this earth for the sole purpose of having women fall hopelessly in love with your good looks and charm, but don't expect me to start drooling. I came here to work, and I can either work with you or against you, it's entirely up to you.'

He looked completely astounded for a moment, but then a reluctant grin spread across his face. 'You certainly don't pull your punches, do you? I'm sorry, I had you figured completely wrong. Most of the single girls who come here to work or on holiday seem to have only one thing on their minds, and that, of course, is matrimony, and the richer the victim is the better.'

Soon a rapport established between them and Felicity found that Geoff could be an amusing companion as he told her stories of some of the patients he had encountered during his term on the island.

'I expect you'll have the usual run of European women coming in to see you with vague complaints,' he said with a return of his old cynicism. 'You'll find that the only thing wrong with them is that they don't have enough to do and too much time to do it in, so they delight in gossip and scandal and imagine they have innumerable things wrong with their health. And they really believe it, too! Most of them develop into acute hypochondriacs by the time they reach forty. Unless they manage to get involved in a love affair, of course. That usually takes their minds off their imaginary aches and pains.'

Felicity laughed at him, but she couldn't help wondering just what had made Geoff so hostile towards her sex. Perhaps in the past one of the women he had so disparagingly described had tried to work her frustrations off on him and he had been hurt in the process.

Mac returned in time to take her back to the bungalow for a light lunch, but he insisted that she stayed with Ellen instead of returning with him to the hospital in the afternoon. When he had gone Ellen explained that anyone with any sense had a siesta in the hottest part of the day, and made her go and rest in her room. Felicity took off her blouse and skirt and lay on her bed in her slip, intending to think about how she would develop the family planning clinics, but she soon fell into a deep and dreamless sleep from which Ellen, looking in a couple of hours later, decided not to disturb her.

When she did finally awaken there was only time to help Ellen to arrange flowers from the garden in large vases which they placed round the living and dining rooms, while Joey hung festoons of coloured lights round the edge of the veranda.

'We'll eat indoors, of course,' Ellen explained. 'But you'll find that most parties tend to gradually gravitate towards the garden in the course of the evening. Barbecue parties are very popular here and Mac and I usually give one or two during the summer, mostly when the boys are home.'

'It sounds fun,' Felicity remarked. 'I've never been to anything like that.'

19

'Then we must be sure and have one very soon before everyone else invites you to theirs.'

'Oh, please, Ellen, I didn't mean to ... I wasn't asking you to ...'

'No, my dear, I know you weren't. But it's about time we gave a real party again. Your coming to live with us has given me a lovely excuse—and Mac can't say a word about it,' she added triumphantly.

Felicity laughed and went to change for dinner. She was undecided what to wear at first, but chose a soft brown shirt dress with a very flared skirt and a belt that fitted snugly round her slim waist. The whiteness of her skin showed through the chiffon material of the long, full sleeves, and Felicity determined to acquire a sun-tan just as soon as she could.

The first of the guests to arrive that evening were Gillian and Colin Marsh, and it took only a swift scrutiny to realise that Gillian was the more dominant personality of the two. She had very short dark hair and thin, almost angular features that gave her a somewhat hungry look, and this, together with the brittle brightness of her smile and the restlessness of her hands as she held both a drink and a cigarette, immediately made Felicity wonder if she was one of Geoff's 'frustrated females'. In comparison her husband appeared to be very quiet, but he gave Felicity a friendly smile and had started to welcome her to Trenaka when Gillian impatiently interrupted him to ask where she had lived in England.

Felicity was answering her when Ellen called her away to meet the other two couples who had just arrived. These were the Lloyds, Hugh and Marion, who came from Cardiff and had lilting Welsh accents that compared favourably with Ellen and Mac's harsher, northern dialect, and Esmé and Charles Sinclair, who had no accent at all. Both of these couples were in their early forties and much nearer to her hosts' age group than her own, and although Felicity found them all very friendly and sociable, she did not have her work in common with them, as had immediately bridged the gap between Mac and herself.

It was with some relief, therefore, that she was introduced to the last guest, David Cameron, who was a bachelor and had obviously been invited as her escort. He greeted her formally but didn't try to monopolise her company, turning to acknowledge the other guests for a while before coming back to Felicity's side with a refilled glass for her.

'Have you seen much of the island yet?' he enquired.

'No, very little, I'm afraid. Ellen was going to take me for a drive this afternoon, but I must have been more tired than I thought and slept for hours.'

'It's the heat. You'll find it very enervating at first.' His face was very tanned and the sun had bleached his fair hair almost white.

'You must be out in the open a lot,' Felicity said politely.

His blue eyes twinkled at her mischievously. 'It does show, doesn't it? I believe it's what is described as "weather-beaten".'

Felicity saw that he was laughing at her and smiled back. The ice broken, they chatted easily until it was time to go in to dinner where conversation became general, except where one or two rather bitchy remarks from Gillian Marsh created little pools of silence that were quickly glossed over by the others. Felicity watched as the other girl took a white flower from the centrepiece and pulled it into a heap of shredded petals with nervous, jerky movements of her fingers.

Coffee was taken on the veranda where Gillian came to sit in the rattan chair beside Felicity's, frankly assessing her.

'That's a pretty little dress you're wearing. I suppose you bought quite a few things in England before you came out here?' Hardly had Felicity had time to acknowledge this before Gillian continued pettishly, 'The shops in Trenaka town are absolutely useless. Most of the clothes are imported and the styles are archaic—all Bermuda shorts and sun-frocks in ghastly colours. I did think of starting a little boutique in the town with really good British clothes, but I wasn't allowed to go ahead with it, of course.'

'Why was that? Didn't your husband want you to take it on?'

'Colin?' Gillian answered in some surprise. 'Good heavens, why should he have anything to say in the matter? No, it was Cecily Steventon—you know, the Governor's wife. The old biddy is terribly old-fashioned and believes that Service wives shouldn't become involved in anything that even remotely smells of "trade". She expects us to spend all our time at endless coffee mornings and cocktail parties, or else doing good works. Why, she had the nerve to suggest that I should go and help out with the West Indians at that ghastly hospital!'

Felicity had to laugh at her. 'Steady on, I *have* to work there, you know.'

Gillian immediately looked contrite. 'Lord, I'm terribly sorry. It must be wretched having to work for a living,' she said, completely unaware of the ambiguity of her statement. 'But please don't take any notice of me. I'm renowned for dropping the proverbial clanger.'

'I'd noticed,' Felicity replied dryly. 'But is Lady Steventon really such a tartar?'

'Yes, she doesn't even like us to mix with the tourists, although heaven knows, there are few enough of those. This place is a real geographical backwater.' Gillian looked at Felicity consideringly. 'We've never even had a professional woman on the island before. I wonder how dear Cecily will react to you,' she said with a touch of malice in her voice.

Deciding to ignore this, Felicity remarked, 'There seems to be a lot of social activity, though. I seem to remember Ellen saying that the Governor had a social secretary— Diane, wasn't it?'

'Diane Cunningham. She's nearly as bad as Lady Steventon. They're related, you know. The Guv's wife is training Diane for her future role in life, especially as she seems to be getting quite serious about Bruce, although personally I think that Cecily has done more to bring that affair about than either of the two principals,' Gillian added with a return to her former bitchiness.

Felicity's pulse was racing as she carefully phrased her next question. 'Her future role in life? That sounds as if it might be something rather important?'

'Lord, yes. Bruce is so ambitious that nothing less than an eventual ambassadorship will satisfy him, and of course dear Diane will make him an absolutely perfect consort if Lady S. has her way. Why Colin can't be a bit more like Bruce, I don't know. I give him every encouragement to attain a higher position, but he's content to just jog placidly along, so we end up in this watershed when we could be in Bermuda or Hong Kong, where there's some real action.'

After a few minutes Felicity realised that once started in this vein Gillian could carry on indefinitely and that she would learn nothing more about her enemy, so, after a polite interval, she excused herself and mingled with the other guests.

The only other piece of interesting information she gleaned that evening was from David Cameron. Felicity had walked a little way into the garden, and turning a corner in the path had come upon a flower-framed arbour with a breathtaking view of the moonlit sea. Grateful to be away from the oppressive warmth of the house, she sat on the stone seat and took long, deep breaths of the heavenly scented air, gazing across the bay to where the lights of the town were reflected in the rippling waters of the harbour. It seemed such a wonderfully peaceful place, as if everyone who lived here must always be happy and contented to work and play in the warmth of the sunlit days and under the clear canopy of the starry nights; as if passions could never flare and crimes never be committed in such a perfect spot. But then she smiled at her own fantasy. She had painted a picture of paradise and there was no paradise on earth, only in the wishful dreams of mortal men and women.

Felicity sighed a little and then gasped with surprise as a voice said to her out of the darkness, 'Why the sigh? Surely you aren't homesick for England already?'

'David! You startled me.'

'Sorry. Mrs Mac thought you might not be feeling quite the thing, so she sent me out to find out if you needed any help.'

'That was kind of her—and of you. I must admit I did find the atmosphere a little overpowering, so I came out to get some fresh air. And I'm so glad I did. I hadn't realised that there was such a lovely view of the sea from here.'

'Yes, it's quite something, isn't it? Do you enjoy water sports?'

'Well, I like swimming, but I've never been sailing or anything.'

'Then you must take the opportunity to learn while you're here. As you like swimming you'll probably find that you enjoy skin-diving too. If you like I could give you some lessons,' he added eagerly.

Felicity smiled at him, liking his open, natural manner. 'Thank you, I think I should like that. Do you go diving very often?'

'Oh, yes, Bruce and I usually go about twice a week if he can get away from the office.'

'Bruce Gresham? I hadn't realised that he was a close friend of yours.'

'I wouldn't say we were very close friends, but we both enjoy the sport, and as it's dangerous to dive alone, we find it convenient to go together.'

'Dangerous! Are there sharks and other horrible creatures, then?' Felicity asked with some alarm.

'No, sharks don't come this far,' he replied with a chuckle. 'The danger lies in having an accident and not having anyone with you to help you, or to go for assistance if necessary. But I do know that if ever I was in a tight spot there's no one else I'd rather have along than Bruce. He's the type you can always rely on in an emergency.'

The conversation had changed then and they had gone back to the house. Shortly afterwards the party had broken up and the guests had taken their leave in a flurry of return invitations. After bidding Mac and Ellen goodnight and thanking them for the party, Felicity quickly prepared for bed and switched off the bedside lamp, but instead of getting into bed she went to the open window and drew back the curtains to look out again in the direction of the town where it lay in a tree-lined valley with the Residency on a promontory behind it.

She had learned two widely differing facts about her enemy: that he had the general reputation of being ruthlessly ambitious in his career, and that he was a good person to have around in a tight corner. Somehow the two facts didn't seem to add up; they described an entirely different kind of man. Felicity puzzled over the problem for a while and then decided that she didn't really have enough to go on. But one thing was becoming abundantly clear. If she wanted to hurt Bruce Gresham—and she most certainly wanted to hurt him—then the way to do it would be to harm him professionally. For although he acted as escort and possible suitor to the Governor's secretary, it would appear that his emotions, if any were involved, were subjugated to his ambitions.

The next two days passed quickly with Felicity gradually becoming more integrated into the pattern of hospital life in the mornings and going for a drive, with an occasional stop for a social call on other Service wives, in the afternoons. Felicity found that they were very curious about her at first, looking on a professional career woman as some new breed of animal. They were interested in her background, and as Felicity wanted to avoid any possibility of involving her mother in anything that might happen in the future, she told them that she had been brought up by an elderly aunt.

On the second afternoon, after Ellen had taken her for a drive and pointed out some of the old slave plantations with their huge white-columned mansions, she drove down to a quiet beach and parked under a shady tree.

'I thought you might like a swim, dear. I wouldn't advise you to go alone, but it's quite all right if you're with me or one of the other wives. My daughter used to get very impatient about it, but it really is much wiser in a small community like this.'

For a moment Felicity thought she had meant because of any possible dangers in the sea, but realised that Ellen was gently telling her that she mustn't go swimming without a chaperone. But Ellen needn't have worried; to Felicity it seemed perfectly natural to be with the older woman as her mother had never let her go anywhere alone anyway.

'I've a surprise for you,' Ellen told her after their swim. 'The Governor is giving a dance on Saturday and we've had a note including you on the invitation. You'll find it a nice place for a dance, but very formal, of course,' she added, with just a trace of regret.

She went on to chatter about other things, but Felicity answered only absentmindedly. A dance at the Residency the day after tomorrow. It would be interesting to meet the Governor and his wife, and even more so to meet Miss Diane Cunningham, who was being groomed to be Bruce Gresham's wife, the wife of a future ambassador. She wondered what the perfect Service wife would look like; someone tall and very regal, she supposed, a woman of immaculate background who was always charming and never made mistakes, someone with as much emotion as a dead fish! Just the sort of person Bruce Gresham deserved!

A sentry saluted smartly as the MacAllisters' car went through the ornate gateway and entered the tree-lined drive leading to the white-painted portico and wide, shallow steps of the Residency. Once inside, Ellen led her to a cloakroom where Felicity was able to give a last critical glance at her reflection. She had chosen a floating chiffon evening dress in muted shades of turquoise that was very feminine and flattering to her young slim figure. Her golden hair she had piled into a Grecian effect and the subtle tones of her make-up enhanced her eyes and lips. Mrs Lambert had always insisted that Felicity be well-groomed and had taken great pains to teach her to choose the right clothes and cosmetics. It had been their one common indulgence.

The ballroom was on the first floor, approached by an immense, sweeping staircase lined with portraits of previous Governors and their ladies. A young uniformed officer, whom Mac introduced as the Governor's aide, awaited them on the landing and ceremoniously announced them. In fact everything was so formal that Felicity almost felt that she ought to curtsey when she was presented to Sir Miles Steventon and had an overwhelming desire to giggle. She looked up and found the Governor looking at her with an answering twinkle in his bushy-browed eyes, and her own gleamed in response.

'Welcome to the islands, Miss Lambert. No, I refuse to call you Doctor. Such a charming young lady should never be denigrated by such a neutral title. I insist that you have a dance with me later. A slow one, because it's so much easier to chat during a slow dance, don't you think?'

Felicity smilingly agreed and turned to meet his wife, an aloof, exquisitely groomed woman who greeted her with gracious condescension. The dancing had already begun and after greeting Gillian and Colin Marsh and other acquaintances, Felicity was soon whisked away by Mac to dance a lively quickstep. The good doctor had more enthusiasm than style, however, and she turned a laughing face up to him as she begged him to be careful of her toes.

'You don't want me to be a patient myself, do you?' she mocked.

'Well, you see, it's not really my dance,' he confided. 'But you should wait until you see me doing some Highland reels, then you'll see what I call dancing. Not this running around the floor like a flock of lost sheep.'

Felicity laughed at his absurdity, her face prettily flushed and her amber eyes dancing with merriment. Suddenly she became aware of being watched and turned her head to see a tall man with broad shoulders encased in a white tuxedo, and lean athletic hips, standing in an archway leading to another room. There was an arrested expression on his tanned, angularly handsome face as his grey eyes followed her, and although Felicity glanced in his direction for only a moment she was instantly aware of every detail of his features.

She went on gaily answering Mac's banter, but her whole body seemed to be one mass of screaming nerves that blinded and deafened her to anything but the few words that kept throbbing through her head. He was here—her enemy! Bruce Gresham was here! The shock of seeing him so unexpectedly when he was not due back on Trenaka until the following week had completely unnerved her. Gropingly she tried to gather her scattered wits. He must have come back earlier than expected, and what more natural than he should come to the Governor's dance.

She dared not look towards him again; there was no need. She had only seen him once before, on that night ten years ago when the police had insisted he come to the police station to clear himself of her mother's accusations. This he had done, completely and contemptuously. He had hardly glanced at Felicity, a thin, leggy and very scared girl of fifteen, standing behind her mother's chair, and she was certain he wouldn't recognise her. But she had known him at once. Although then, at twenty-five, he had been thinner, less of a man, his face had been irrevocably stamped on her memory for ever.

CHAPTER TWO

THE quickstep ended at last and Mac took the opportunity to perform introductions to several of the other guests, but soon they were joined by David Cameron who claimed Felicity for the next dance. He held her carefully, like a piece of Dresden china, as he guided her round the room.

'Don't forget your promise to come diving,' he reminded her. 'How about tomorrow for your first lesson?'

'That will be fine. I don't think Ellen and Mac have anything planned.' Felicity tried to reply naturally, but her voice felt tight in her throat and it took some courage to direct a quick sideways glance at the archway, but it was empty. He had gone, and she was able to relax a little and still the wild fluttering beat of her heart.

When the dance ended David led her to the side of the floor and continued to make arrangements for the following day, but they were interrupted by someone who came up behind Felicity. She didn't have to turn round to know who it was. Some deep inner sensitivity had already warned her even before Bruce Gresham spoke.

'David! How are you? I see that you've managed to steal a march on me while I've been away, but now that I'm back I must insist that you introduce me and allow me to make up for lost time.'

Felicity raised her eyes and found cool grey ones looking quizzically down into her own. With a somewhat rueful grin David did as he was asked, and as Felicity's hand was taken in the firm grasp of her enemy she felt herself shiver uncontrollably.

'Really, David, what can you be thinking of? You

haven't even got Miss Lambert a drink,' he pointed out.

David flushed slightly and hurried off to the bar leaving Felicity feeling desperately alone, as if there was no one else in the room but herself and her brother's murderer. And he had contrived that it should be so; sending David away as easily as a master ordering a schoolboy. But why? Felicity raised her head and found him looking at her with a puzzled expression.

'You know, Miss Lambert, I can't help feeling that we've met somewhere before.'

Panic overwhelmed her. He mustn't remember, he mustn't! or all would be lost before it had even begun. Fear gave her strength and she answered in sheer desperation with the first thing that came into her head. Summoning up a look of amused disdain, she said lightly, 'Really, Mr Gresham, I'd heard that these islands were backward, but I hadn't expected the inhabitants to use such a prehistoric approach as that!'

For a moment he looked completely taken aback, but then a look of rueful amusement came into his eyes. 'It does sound rather like a line from a very bad "B" film, doesn't it? And I'm afraid that it can't be true. I've a feeling that if I'd met you before I would certainly have remembered you, Miss Lambert. No, the name doesn't ring a bell either.'

Felicity breathed a small, silent sigh of relief. No, he wouldn't have remembered the name; her mother had decided to use her maiden name soon after they had moved from Alnswick. Then it had been Callison, now and for ever it was Lambert.

He was still looking at her thoughtfully, but Felicity raised her chin defiantly and steadily returned his scrutiny, although her hands were two tightly balled fists hidden in the folds of her gown. Mercifully David returned with the drinks and she was able to take a glass from him without anyone noticing the red marks on her palms where her nails had dug deeply in.

'Bruce, would you mind if I borrowed your spare air

tanks tomorrow? I've promised to teach Felicity to dive and my spare tanks need repairing.'

'Of course. Where do you propose to dive?'

'The usual place, off Muleteers Beach. I'll pick them up from you on my way round tomorrow.'

He was about to continue when Lady Steventon walked over to them accompanied by a girl of about thirty with brown, elegantly coiffured hair and a pleasant face, but with rather harassed eyes.

'Dr Lambert, I don't think you've met my cousin, Miss Diane Cunningham?' Was Felicity mistaken when she thought that Lady Steventon had emphasised the 'doctor'?

After the formal introduction Lady Steventon drew Bruce and David into conversation while the two girls exchanged polite platitudes, then their hostess adroitly took Felicity away to meet some late arrivals. Supper was served in a separate room where Felicity joined David and the MacAllisters and their friends, while she noticed that Bruce sat at a table with the Steventons, several senior officials and, of course, Diane, who sat next to him and seemed to be holding him in close conversation, from the way that she leant towards him and looked eagerly up into his face.

Back in the ballroom Felicity had her promised dance with Sir Miles and found him a cheery, uncomplicated man who tended to treat her like a little girl and refused to take seriously the fact that she was a dedicated career woman.

'Nonsense, m'dear,' he insisted. 'You'll soon be taking one of these bachelors off my hands and setting up home for yourself.'

Felicity didn't try to argue with him; she had met the type all too often before to attempt a rational discussion. The heat was much more than she was used to and she made her way over to the balcony windows which were wide open to the garden, and stood there gently fanning herself with a pretty paper fan that Ellen had lent her for the evening.

'Miss Lambert. May I have this dance?' Felicity turned to see Bruce Gresham standing close beside her, and suddenly she knew quite definitely that she couldn't dance with him. She just couldn't bear to let this man hold her in his arms when all the time she hated him so much that she wanted to make him grovel at her feet and beg forgiveness for the years of suffering he had caused her mother. Instead she replied coolly, 'No, thank you, Mr Gresham. I find the heat rather enervating.'

But he didn't take his dismissal and go; instead he put his hand under her elbow and drew her out on to the balcony. 'Then you'll probably enjoy a stroll in the gardens.' Firmly he led her to the end of the balustrade and Felicity saw that there were stone steps leading down to a path running through the landscaped gardens. They walked a little way in silence and then she gave an involuntary exclamation of delight as they passed under an archway of flowering hibiscus and came upon a fountain lit by coloured lights under the water, while a stone cherub played a flute atop his pedestal in the centre.

'There's a tradition that if you throw a coin into the fountain and make a wish it will come true,' he told her enigmatically. 'Here, I'll give you a coin so that you can wish.' He took her hand and placed a small coin in the palm, closing her fingers over it.

Slowly Felicity raised her head and looked at him where he sat nonchalantly on the fountain's edge. 'Aren't you going to make a wish?'

He shook his head decisively. 'I don't depend on the fates. If I want something I do everything in my power to make sure I get it. Throwing coins is just a profitable sideline for the gardener; in fact I wouldn't be surprised if he hadn't invented the idea. But you haven't made your wish yet.'

'I don't think I want to.'

'Are you afraid it won't come true?' His tone was mocking.

'No. I'm afraid that it might! Shall we go in now?' She

turned without a backward glance and retraced her steps to the ballroom.

There was little sleep for Felicity that night, but she managed a friendly smile when David called to collect her the next morning. The whole population of Trenaka seemed to be outside their homes as they drove in his big blue American convertible across the island to the beach he had chosen for their first lesson. Already children were playing cricket on the pitches that seemed to be marked out in every village, while women spread husked rice to dry in the sun. Occasionally they had to slow down to allow herds of sheep or goats to move off the road when David sounded his horn; they were not penned in at all and wandered at will looking for more succulent pasturage.

David carefully negotiated a steeply descending side road, and Felicity gave a gasp of pure delight as he pulled up at a small cove of sun-bleached coral sand. Palm trees provided stretches of shade and there were rock pools left behind by the tide with large ornate shells which shone with a myriad colours and boomed with the sound of the sea when Felicity lifted them to her ear. Her face as glowing as that of a child, she turned to David to show him her finds and found him watching her with a pensive expression in his eyes. Immediately she became brisk and started to unload the car so that he had to help her. She hadn't given any thought as yet to David as a person; only knowing that she would gladly accept him as a friend, but wanting no other, closer relationship to develop to complicate her objective on Trenaka. Her personal feelings must be kept strictly under control until she had found a way to be revenged on Bruce.

First David explained the equipment to her, but said that she must start with just snorkel and mask before she could progress to the air tanks. They waded out in the cove until the sea came up to Felicity's chest and then David showed her how to swim with her head under the water and

33

breathe through the snorkel tube. She found it awkward at first and tended to forget to breathe, but gradually she mastered it. When she opened her eyes below the surface she gasped in surprise and swallowed water; the sea had suddenly come alive and she gazed in fascination at the brightly coloured fish that darted along the sea-bed, busy about their constant task of seeking food.

When she was breathing naturally and felt at home with the snorkel, David led her to some rocks where they could look down on the shellfish that made their homes in the hollows and crevices. Felicity was so enthralled by this new underwater world that she would gladly have stayed all day, but David smilingly told her that she must take things gently at first and they made their way back to the shore.

The warmth of the sun felt heavenly as Felicity waded out of the sea and she put her hands up to take off her mask and bathing hat, shaking her head so that her hair fell tumbling about her shoulders and lifting her face to feel the sun's caress. Slowly she opened her eyes and started to walk through the shallows, then she stopped, tense, her nerves jangling. Bruce Gresham was leaning casually against his car, quietly smoking a cigarette. He was dressed in a cream loose-knit shirt and well-cut shorts and looked bronzed and masculine as he stood there, waiting for them to come to him.

'Sorry I wasn't at home when you called, David. Had to go over to the harbour in rather a hurry, so I thought I'd bring the tanks along for you myself.'

'Thanks, that was good of you.' Bruce made no effort to leave, so David added, without great enthusiasm, 'We're just going to take a breather; stay and have a drink with us?'

'I should be delighted—if Miss Lambert doesn't object?'

Felicity couldn't see his eyes behind the dark sunglasses that he wore, but suddenly she became aware of her wet swimsuit clinging to her and outlining every detail of her body, although she hadn't given it a thought when David looked at her.

'Of course not,' she replied politely. 'It was kind of you to bring the tanks.'

They shared out the drinks David had brought and chatted together for a while. Then Bruce pulled off his shirt to reveal a hard, smooth chest and strong, muscled arms. 'Here,' he said, holding out the shirt to Felicity, 'put this on. If you stay in the sun any longer you'll start to burn.'

'But I've only been sitting here for about twenty minutes!'

'That's plenty for the first time,' he said firmly. 'Put it on.'

Felicity looked rather indignantly into his eyes and knew then, with a sinking heart, that this man would always be able to force his will on her. She felt suddenly very vulnerable and alone, but then her natural resilience came surging back and she answered coolly, 'Thank you, but I have a beach-wrap in the car.'

'I'll get it for you,' David volunteered at once, and went away to fetch it.

She didn't look to see Bruce's reaction but gave David a wonderful smile when he returned. She couldn't be sure, but she certainly thought she heard Bruce give a low mocking laugh, then decided that she must have been mistaken. Soon afterwards he took his leave, and David continued with her lessons by making her put on the tanks and get used to their cumbersome weight before trying them out in the water. Felicity found the unaccustomed exercise rather exhausting, and although she had thoroughly enjoyed her introduction to this new sport, was glad enough when David called a halt and took her home, arranging for another lesson the following week if Felicity's commitments at the hospital allowed.

Dr Geoffrey Lord lived in a small bungalow in the hospital grounds so that he was on hand should any emergency arise

35

during the nights. Felicity was working full time at the hospital now, but as there was a quiet period one afternoon he had invited her over to the bungalow for a drink and to inspect a painting he had acquired.

'It's by a local artist—a French chap who called here for a few hours on a cruise about twenty years ago and liked the place so much that he just left the ship and has been here ever since. He's getting on a bit now, but he's still one of our most colourful characters.'

Felicity took the picture from him and balanced it on a chair at the back of the veranda, stepping back so that she could get a better perspective. The canvas was only about two feet square, but the artist had filled it with the teeming life and colour of the town square on market day.

'It really *is* Trenaka town, isn't it? He must have a marvellous eye for detail—yet everything is suggested rather than clearly defined,' she said enthusiastically.

'You have good taste.' The voice from behind her made her turn quickly to see Bruce standing at the foot of the steps. She hadn't heard him approach across the grass and her dismay at his sudden appearance made her start to tremble with emotion. He came up the steps and stood beside her to look at the picture more closely.

'Yes,' he continued. 'That's one of the old boy's better works, probably painted about ten years ago, I should think. His hands are rather unsteady now, I'm afraid.' He turned to Geoff. 'Where did you pick it up?'

'Oh, no, you don't,' Geoff laughed. 'I refuse to reveal the secret. Find your own masterpieces, Bruce.'

Bruce wasn't put out. 'I shall find out, never fear. You can't keep something like that up your sleeve for long. Do you like the painting?' he asked Felicity.

'Very much. I should like to find one to take back to England with me before I leave.'

'Talking of leaving already? Your tour of duty is for three years, isn't it?' He raised his eyebrow quizzically.

'Yes, of course,' she said lightly, annoyed with herself

for having slipped up. 'But if Geoff is going to snap up all the pictures that come on the market, it will probably take me all that time to find one.'

'Who knows, perhaps you might fall in love and decide to stay—with Trenaka, of course,' Bruce added after a short but definite pause.

Felicity looked at him with a slight frown. Was he deliberately trying to tease her? She could read nothing from his expression which was completely impassive, so she reverted to her cool professional manner and said, 'You must be waiting to speak to Dr Lord, so I'll get back to the hospital.'

She turned to go down the steps, but he put his hand on her arm and stopped her. 'But it was you I came to see, Miss Lambert. I've brought a car over for you. Come and see what you think of it.'

Every nerve was aflame as, with his hand still under her elbow, he led her towards the front of the hospital. Felicity could stand it no longer; she raised her arm as if to straighten her hair and moved slightly away from his side as they walked, so that when she put her arm down again they were no longer touching. If he noticed the manoeuvre he made no comment, but a swift glance showed her an odd little quirk at the side of his mouth.

'Here it is,' he said. 'What do you think of it?'

'It' was a shiny new red Mini with black upholstery and a canvas roof that could be rolled back to let in more air. Felicity expressed her approval and he put the keys in her hand.

'Good. Get in and we'll go for a spin.'

She stared at him in consternation. Going for a drive with this man was the last thing she wanted. 'I'm afraid I can't leave the hospital at the moment; I'm on duty.'

'Nonsense, Geoff will take care of any emergency that may crop up.'

Felicity began to get annoyed. 'If I were a man would you bother to see how I handled a car?'

He grinned. 'Probably not, but as most women are notoriously unmechanical, I should like to assure myself that you are able to at least find the correct gear. After all, I should hate to have to indent for a new gearbox before the car has been run in,' he added outrageously. Going to the driver's side, he opened the door and held it for her. Felicity glared back at him defiantly and his voice was mocking as he said, 'You may think me every kind of a male chauvinist you like, Miss Lambert, but I'm going to insist on accompanying you, so we may as well get it over.'

For a few moments she continued to defy him, then shrugged and climbed into the car. He shut the door for her and went round to the passenger side, but she ignored him as she adjusted her seat and made sure that the mirror was at the right angle for her. Calmly she fastened her seat belt and inspected the controls. She had driven Minis before and was quietly confident of her ability. Without waiting for him to speak, she started the engine and drove towards the road that led away from the town.

Concentrating on the unfamiliar controls and terrain she forgot the man beside her, so that when he told her to take a turning to the left it made her jump and the car swerved a little. She could feel him watching her and the ghastly realisation of whom she was with came rushing back, making her grip the steering wheel until her knuckles shone white. Biting her lip, she managed to follow his directions and presently, after they had climbed a steep hill, they came out into an open space and he told her to pull up on a piece of ground at the edge of the road.

She turned off the engine and deliberately made herself relax. 'Tell me, do you always deliver cars in person? I thought you were one of the most senior officials on the island.'

'Not usually, but I decided to make an exception in your case.'

'I'm flattered. And did I pass my driving test?' Her voice was brittle.

'With flying colours. But why so tense? I don't bite, you know.' His voice was oddly gentle, persuasive. He was so tall and broad that his presence seemed to fill the little car.

'Did we stop here for any special reason?' she asked coldly, not facing him.

Bruce looked at her for a moment and then answered in his normal tone. 'Yes, I thought you might like to see the view.'

Getting out of the car, he came round and opened Felicity's door so that she had to get out. Without touching her, he led her to a waist-high wall at the edge of the hillside and looking out she could see spread out before her a panoramic view of the coastline that was breathtaking in its beauty. For a few minutes she was too spellbound to speak, then she said slowly, 'Now I know why the French painter didn't want to leave.'

He lit cigarettes for them both and leaned back against the wall looking at her and not the view.

'How big is the island?' she asked him.

'Roughly fifty miles long by about twenty-five wide. Most of the islands in the group are physically like this, with a central mountain range that falls sharply to cliffs or a coastal plain.'

Felicity turned and looked behind her up to the mountains with their sharply serrated ridges that branched out and then fell away to the thick greenness of the forests at their feet. Over to the right were the cragged walls of grey cliffs that dropped sheer to the pounding surf below.

'Isn't that a wreck over by the rocks?' she asked with interest, pointing in the direction of the cliffs.

'Yes, it ran on to the reef in a hurricane some years ago. There are several wrecks around the island that make good practice grounds for underwater diving. We must explore them when David has given you a few more lessons.'

Did he include David in that 'we'? Felicity wondered.

'It's getting late. I really ought to get back.'

He didn't attempt to detain her, merely saying, 'There's

no point in going back to the hospital. Perhaps you could drop me off at my house before going on to the MacAllisters'?'

'Yes, of course. But you'll have to direct me. I don't know where you live.'

He raised a quizzical eyebrow. 'You shouldn't have much difficulty finding it. I live only a short distance away from you. We're almost neighbours, in fact.'

'Oh.' Felicity could find nothing more to say at this piece of news. She just hoped that Bruce wasn't in the habit of dropping in for neighbourly visits on Mac and Ellen.

His house was a two-storied building set well back from the road and shaded by palms, banana trees and golden-blossomed logwoods.

'Would you care to come in for a drink?' he asked, his hand on the door handle.

'Not right now, thanks,' she replied, wishing that he would hurry up and go so that she could start to think coherently again.

The mocking smile that was beginning to be almost familiar was again on his lips. 'You know, Miss Lambert, I've noticed that whenever I invite you to do something, you consistently say "No". Hardly the polite thing to do for a young lady as well brought up as I'm sure you are. I wonder why it is? Can it be because you're shy—or is it because you're afraid to say "Yes"?'

Felicity felt her heart thumping and she dared not look at him. 'Really, Mr Gresham, you're making something out of nothing. And now, if you'll excuse me, I have to go home to get ready for an invitation I *did* accept.'

'Touché!' He held up his hands in mock surrender, and getting out of the car watched her as she drove down the road to the MacAllisters'.

Had he been teasing her? Felicity wondered as she showered and changed. She mustn't let it become too obvious that she disliked him, for she still hadn't thought of a way to destroy his reputation. What had seemed so easy to plan back in England now seemed impossible to execute here in Trenaka. How did one go about ruining a man who apparently had no weaknesses? Perhaps he had hidden vices, thought Felicity with forlorn hope. Well, if he had she would never find out by being unfriendly towards him. She sighed, and wondered if her mother realised just what she was going through. Every letter Felicity received from her was full of questions asking her what action she was going to take and when.

David called to collect her at eight o'clock, telling her that he had booked a table at a restaurant for dinner. He seemed pleased that he had been able to make a reservation as he said the place was extremely popular. Felicity asked him where it was, but he chose to be mysterious.

'It's a surprise. Wait and see,' he teased her.

Felicity laughingly humoured him and instead told him about her new Mini.

'Bruce brought it himself?' he exclaimed in surprise.

'He seemed to doubt my ability to change gear,' she told him dryly.

'I'm sure you're a very good driver,' David said consolingly.

'Then you wouldn't mind me trying my hand at this car?' Felicity remarked innocently, indicating the huge, shiny and much-loved car they were travelling in. Then she laughed as David paled beneath his sun-tan.

He grinned back ruefully. 'I really fell into that one, didn't I? Here we are.' He parked the car and helped her out. 'Now shut your eyes until I tell you to open them.'

Obediently she allowed him to guide her along for several yards and then turn a corner. 'Now!' he said triumphantly.

Felicity opened her eyes, not knowing what to expect. They were standing on a wooden jetty that stretched some way out to sea and moored at the end was a large old sailing ship with two rows of gun ports, a figurehead of a partially clothed and very voluptuous lady, and, flying from the masthead, a huge flag with the sinister skull-and-crossbones emblem. She turned to David in delighted amazement. 'This is a restaurant?'

'Yes, it's called the Jolly Roger. Some enterprising people had the idea of building a replica of a pirateer as a nightclub. Come on, let's go on board.'

As they got nearer they could hear the beat of a steel band, and once aboard and down the companionway to the deck below, they found the whole area crowded with tables of customers and hurrying waiters dressed as pirates and some people were already dancing in the small space provided near the band. An eye-patched pirate led them to their table and David helped her to choose from the huge, double-paged menu. Eagerly Felicity looked around her; she had never been to a night-club before and she found the whole experience exciting. She was especially fascinated by the band in their gaily coloured costumes with yards of ruffles in the sleeves. Their instruments were just steel drums of various lengths, but the range of tone was complete.

'They're made from forty-gallon oil-drums.' David told her. 'The bottoms are cut off and the tops stretched by beating them into a convex shape. They call them pans.'

'Are there always six players in a band?'

'Gosh, no. Some of the bands are much bigger. You should hear them at carnival time. They practise for weeks beforehand and then have a great competition to find the best.'

The food was delicious although the service was a little slow, but Felicity enjoyed listening to the calypso singers in the cabaret. David introduced her to a rum drink called Planter's Punch, which he informed her was the staple diet on the island.

'Wow! That's really potent stuff,' Felicity exclaimed when she tried it. 'I've an idea it might replace the anaesthetic at the hospital.'

'It would certainly be more popular,' David laughed. 'Although I think you'll find the natives are pretty immune to it.'

'Are all the drinks made from rum?' Felicity enquired as she sipped it rather gingerly.

'Most of them. It's the main product of the West Indies, you see.'

Afterwards they danced and later David suggested a walk on the upper deck. It was fun strolling around imagining what a real pirate ship would have been like and examining the one or two genuine cannon that had been preserved and mounted at the stern.

David looked along a gun and remarked, 'Do you know, I think they've deliberately sighted this gun so that it's aiming straight at the Residency.'

They looked towards the shore at the twinkling lights of the town and Felicity almost wished the gun *had* been loaded so that she could blow her enemy into oblivion. She sighed with vexation; why did he have to come into her mind now, when she was out enjoying herself, away from Bruce Gresham and all he stood for? She felt cold suddenly despite the close heat of the night. From then on all the pleasure in the evening was gone, but somehow she managed to put on an act of gaiety for David's sake. It wasn't his fault that her conscience had reawakened itself.

The following day was busier than usual at the hospital with an emergency operation in the afternoon. Immediately afterwards the two male doctors were washing up while Felicity locked away the instruments they had been using.

'I've left my notebook over at the bungalow,' Geoff remarked, wiping his hands. 'I'll just go across and get it.'

'Leave it until I've discussed this case with you, will you?' Mac said. 'I want your opinion on the dosage of drug we should prescribe.'

'It won't take a minute,' the younger man interrupted. 'And I shall need it for my reports.'

'Let Felicity get it for you if it's that important,' Mac said rather testily, obviously thinking that Geoff was fussing unduly.

'Oh, but . . .'

'I'll go,' Felicity assured them, and without waiting for a reply she left the building by a door leading into the garden.

The bungalow was set apart from the hospital complex and screened from it by surrounding trees and shrubs. In her flat, rubber soled hospital shoes she crossed the veranda and entered the living room. Geoff kept his notebook in the top drawer of his desk, which squeaked when she opened it.

A rather exasperated voice from an inner room said, 'Geoff, you might have let me know you were going to be delayed. I've been waiting here for ages.' And Gillian Marsh walked into the room.

It would have been difficult to know who was the most surprised. Both girls stared at each other in consternation, but of the two it was probably Felicity who was the most embarrassed. She picked up the notebook and said rather inadequately, 'Geoff had to help Mac with an emergency op.'

'Oh!' With an almost visible effort Gillian pulled herself together and said with a bright, false smile, 'I had an appointment with him. Just the renewal of a prescription really.' Seeing the question in Felicity's eyes, she added hastily, 'I never go to the hospital—it's something about them—the smell, I suppose. Will he be long? We always see him privately, you know.'

She was too tense; too loquacious; her fingers never still.

'Yes, I'm afraid he'll be some time. Perhaps I can ask him to make another appointment for you?'

'Oh, no,' hastily. 'I'll phone him, or else get Colin to drop in.'

Felicity nodded, and picking up the notebook, turned to leave. Had Geoff left the book purposely so that he would have an excuse to go to Gillian? Felicity didn't want to even think about it.

'Wait!' Gillian's voice stopped her. 'Perhaps you could give me a prescription, as you're here. It's just that I'm organising a party and I get awfully uptight on these occasions. If you could give me some tranquillisers ...?'

Felicity looked at her doubtfully, but the poor girl certainly needed something to calm her down. 'My prescription pad is in the office,' she explained.

'I'll come with you.' Gillian had apparently forgotten her phobia about hospitals.

Once in the office, Felicity quickly wrote out a prescription. 'But remember, don't take them with alcohol and don't take more than the prescribed dose,' she warned.

'No, I won't,' Gillian assured her, and hurried away.

Felicity sighed, wondering if Geoff knew what he was letting himself in for. Edwina poked her head round the door. 'Time for a cup of tea?'

'Yes, please, Edwina. Why is it you always know just when I need it?'

'Comes of long experience,' Edwina replied with a smile as she poured them each a cup.

This little afternoon ritual had become a pleasant interlude in Felicity's day. She found herself able to relax with Edwina and learned a lot about the islanders from talking to her. Edwina had been born in England, but her parents had emigrated to the West Indies when she was quite young. She had been married several years ago and she and her husband had gone to live in America because he had thought they would get on better there, but after obtaining a job as a truck driver her husband had been killed in a freeway accident and Edwina had returned to Trenaka to take up the job at the hospital. She lived quietly and didn't mix with the Service crowd, but she had no bitterness about the past and always had a cheerful, smiling face for staff and patients alike. Felicity admired her tremendously.

After dinner that evening the telephone rang and Mac

went to answer it, but after only a short conversation he told Felicity that the call was for her.

'Hallo, Felicity, this is Gillian. I just thought I'd let you know that I've fixed the date for my barbecue party for the twenty-sixth. You will be able to come, won't you?'

'Thank you, I believe I'm free that weekend.'

'Oh, good.' Gillian paused. 'Felicity, about this afternoon; I wonder if you'd mind not mentioning my visit to the hospital to Mac? He might resent the fact that we prefer Geoff as our doctor.'

'I'm sure he wouldn't, but I shall do as you wish, of course.'

'Thanks,' the older girl sounded relieved. 'Well, don't forget the twenty-sixth, everyone is coming.'

As she put the phone down, Felicity wondered just who 'everyone' included. Not David, for one, because he had been instructed to visit several of the lesser islands whose crops were suffering from some form of blight. He had been rather despondent about the trip as it meant that Felicity would miss her weekly diving lesson just as she was becoming proficient, but he hoped to be back in two or three weeks' time at the latest.

However much Felicity would miss the lessons, she wasn't altogether sorry that David had been sent away, because without the enjoyable distraction of his company she would have more time to concentrate on her other reason for coming to the island. As she lay awake in bed that night listening to the whistle of the tree frogs in the garden, she tried in vain to think of a solution to the problem. She realised that she must involve Bruce in such a terrible scandal that it could never be lived down, and she had come to the conclusion that there were only four ways in which an official could have his career entirely ruined beyond any hope of redemption. These were to be a thief, an alcoholic, to have a brazen affair with another Service man's wife, or to flaunt a woman as his mistress.

But how on earth was she to bring any of these about?

Bruce was obviously not a thief, drank only in moderation and was involved only in a perfectly natural and rather lukewarm association with Diane Cunningham. And if he had a mistress he would take darn good care that no one ever found out about it.

It seemed only minutes after Felicity had at last fallen asleep that she was woken abruptly by a bright flash of light. Startled, she sat up in bed and the next second there came a great clap of thunder that reverberated all around the house. It was only a thunderstorm. She lay back on her pillows and listened to the great cracks that echoed off the mountains and watched the distorted shadows on the walls thrown by the lightning flashes. The storm passed on as quickly as it had come, leaving behind only the sweet smell of a garden after rain, and slowly the realisation came to her that fate had brought her there and just as surely that same fate would show her just how to destroy her enemy. She wouldn't worry about it any more. When the time came she would know what to do.

It was barely dawn when she was roused from a deep sleep by Mac pounding on her door. 'Felicity! Wake up. There's an emergency on Sancreed. We've got to get down to the harbour.'

Quickly Felicity jumped out of bed and, after a hasty toilet, pulled on a dress before joining Mac in the diningroom where he was drinking a cup of coffee served by a sleepy-eyed maid.

'Here, lass,' he said, passing her a cup, 'drink up while I get the car out.'

Soon they were speeding towards the harbour where the hospital boat was moored. This was a large motor launch fitted up for every type of emergency and equipped with cot beds for the transportation of very sick patients from the smaller islands to the hospital. Felicity had been shown round the boat but had not yet been out on her.

'What happened?' she asked Mac as the crew threw off the mooring lines and they made their way out to sea.

'Lightning hit a tree and it fell on to some houses. No one was killed, fortunately, but several have broken bones and crushed limbs. Our equipment should be in order, but we'd better check again, to be on the safe side.'

The island of Sancreed was only about fifty miles from Trenaka and the launch was capable of high speeds, so they had barely finished their preparations before Joey put his head into the sickbay and told them that it was in sight.

'Is Joey part of your crew?' Felicity asked in surprise.

'Yes, he's daft about boats. The captain is his cousin, and he also brings along his young brother who's as bad as he is, so it's quite a family affair.'

The resident official on Sancreed was waiting for them at the jetty with a car and drove them to a small clinic in the largest village. A plump, motherly figure bustled towards them, her brown face creased in a worried frown as she told them the details of the worst cases. Grimly and professionally the two physicians set to work to mend the broken bones and stitch the ghastly wounds. Most of them were routine, but one poor man had had his leg so badly crushed that they eventually decided that they would have to amputate.

'I'm reluctant to perform the operation here,' Mac told her. 'I would far rather take him back to Trenaka so that he can have all the benefits of our hospital equipment. Felicity, would you mind if I left you behind here to finish up the rest of the lesser injuries and to keep an eye on the patients for a few days? There are rather more of them than I expected and it would save me keep coming backwards and forwards every day to make sure they're all okay.'

'Of course.'

'You're sure you don't mind, lassie?'

'No, I shall enjoy being "in charge". And it will give me an opportunity to start a family planning clinic here.'

'You're a good lass. I'll get Ellen to send you over some clothes by the motor boat later in the day.'

Soon he and his patient were gone, leaving Felicity to supervise putting broken legs into traction and arranging transport for those well enough to go home. It was well into the afternoon before she had finished writing up her notes on each patient, and an ominous noise in her tummy reminded her that she hadn't eaten all day. She went in search of Sister Phillips, the resident nurse, and was soon served with a fluffy omelette and green salad with a large dish of fruit to follow. Felicity took the tray outside on to the veranda and ate her meal looking out over the lush green hillsides and sparkling coral beaches of this lovely island.

Thinking back on her few weeks in the West Indies, she realised that this was one of the few times when she had been alone. Always there had been the staff and patients at the hospital, or the MacAllisters at the bungalow. It was not the done thing for a white woman to go out unescorted, and her only solitary ventures had been into town on short shopping trips.

Her meal finished, she rose and strolled down a quiet road through the surrounding fields. It was very hot and she knew she shouldn't go out in the sun without a hat, but she didn't care; the sun felt good on her bare head. A large lizard sat on a stone by the side of the road and watched her with large, unblinking eyes as she walked by. All round her the air was heavy with the noise of countless crickets that made their homes in the long yellow grass. Soon she reached the beach where she took off her shoes and walked along through the soft sand. She would have liked to take off her dress and swim out in the inviting coolness of the ocean, but there were natives fishing with nets in the shallows further along, so she contented herself with paddling in the tiny wavelets at the water's edge. A beautiful shell, more intricate and colourful than any she had found on Trenaka, caught her eye and she picked it up to take back with her. Looking at her watch, she reluctantly put on her shoes and walked back up the road to the clinic and her patients.

As the clinic came in sight she noticed a man sitting on the veranda, and was suddenly aware of the beating of her heart as Bruce Gresham rose to greet her.

'Don't you know you shouldn't go out in the hottest part of the day without a hat?' he said brusquely.

'I haven't noticed you wearing one,' Felicity retorted immediately.

'I'm used to the climate, but someone with a skin as fair as yours could get sunstroke in no time.'

Felicity, whose skin had begun to acquire a honey-golden tan, decided to ignore this remark and said pointedly, 'Did you wish to see me about something?'

There was an almost imperceptible pause before he answered. 'I came over to see about repairing the damage done by the storm, and Mac asked me to bring some clothes over for you.'

'Thank you. That was kind of you.'

'How long do you think you'll have to stay here?'

'Not very long. Most of the patients will be able to go home in a few days and the Sister should be able to cope by herself after that.'

'Then we'll be able to keep each other company. I'm staying on Sancreed myself until the repair work is carried out.' He paused, then added deliberately, 'Perhaps you would care to have dinner with me tonight?'

Speechlessly Felicity raised her eyes to his and found him watching her speculatively, as though waiting for her to make a hurried excuse. She remembered her thought that fate would find a way for her. Perhaps this was the way? Perhaps this was the time?

'Thank you. I shall look forward to that,' she managed to reply in a small, strangled voice. Then she turned and hurried into the clinic before she could see his reaction.

CHAPTER THREE

THE clothes Bruce had brought for her had been put in a spare bedroom, and as she unpacked them that evening she was glad the day had been a busy one, for it had left her no time to worry about the night ahead. She hung her things on hangers and was surprised to find that Ellen had packed an evening dress in the suitcase. Now why had she done that? Felicity wondered. Because she knew Bruce would be on Sancreed and that he would ask her to go out with him; or because Bruce had told Ellen to pack one? Felicity's mouth set in a determined line. Mr Bruce Gresham was just too sure of himself, and it was going to give her great pleasure to finally put him in his place! Then she sighed; first she had to get through this evening.

She put on the burnt-orange coloured halter-necked dress that Ellen had packed and picked up a crocheted shawl to put round her shoulders. Taking a last critical look in the mirror she noticed the tiny pulse beating in her neck, a sure sign of nerves. Her eyes were bright, their golden flecks enhanced by the colour of her dress, and she felt almost lightheaded with apprehension. Her reflection stared back at her and she thought inconsequentially: if hating a man has this effect on me, what on earth would loving one do to me?

There was a soft knock on the door and a little coloured girl told her that Bruce had arrived. Immediately her heart began to beat faster and she forcibly took herself in hand and stood quietly for a few moments until she had conquered her panic and could walk out calmly to

51

meet him, with a polite smile on her face and a greeting on her lips.

He was dressed in a white tuxedo that emphasised his tan and showed off the broad width of his shoulders. His grey eyes looked her over appreciatively as she walked towards him and he took her arm to help her down the steps and into the waiting car.

'I'm afraid this vehicle isn't as comfortable as David's American job, but there aren't a great many available on Sancreed. I borrowed this one from the Government Office.'

'Please don't worry, it's really very comfortable.' Felicity studiously ignored the gathering dusk to scan the terrain through the window and avoided looking at him.

'If you look on the back seat you'll find something for you.'

Then Felicity did look at him, but he was negotiating a tricky stretch of road. Slowly she reached over and picked up the oblong white box that was lying on the seat. It was bound with a bow of yellow silk ribbon and she suddenly felt a strong reluctance to untie it.

'It isn't Pandora's box,' he said lightly, noticing her hesitation. 'Go ahead, open it. I'm not the practical joker type, if that's what you're worrying about.'

Felicity managed a laugh that sounded cracked and brittle even to her own ears.

The silken ribbon lay in a golden pool on her lap as she took off the lid and unfolded some tissue paper and then, unexpectedly, a layer of soft moss. An orchid lay there in its cool bed, its beautiful deep-brown petals glistening in the half-light, and Felicity knew then why it was the most expensive and sought after of flowers. She gave a little gasp of surprise and pleasure, then very carefully lifted out the bloom to smell its heady perfume.

'Oh, thank you,' she said with real gratitude, conscious only of the beauty of the gift he had given her. 'It's exquisite. I've never been given an orchid before,' she added naïvely. 'Do they sell them on the island? I shouldn't have thought there was a florist in such a small place.'

They had come to a small fishing village and now Bruce pulled on to the quayside and parked the car. 'There isn't. They grow wild on the side of the mountain, near a waterfall.'

'Did you get someone to climb up there for it?'

'No, I went up for it myself.' He paused as if expecting her to say something, but Felicity hastily buried her face in the orchid. 'You see, I thought this was rather a special occasion.' He took the flower from her nerveless fingers. 'After all, it is the first time you've ever said "Yes" to me.'

Felicity stole a quick glance at him and saw an amused smile on his face. 'I'm afraid I don't have a pin to fasten it with,' she said, her voice losing its spontaneous warmth of a few moments ago.

'A government official is always prepared,' he misquoted, and produced two pins from his pocket. 'Would you like me to fasten it on for you?'

Felicity looked down at the thin shoulder straps of her dress that plunged to her firm young breasts, and said hastily, 'No, thank you, I can manage,' and fastened it high on her shoulder so that she only had to turn her head to smell its heady scent.

'Is this where we're going to eat?' she asked as he helped her out of the car.

'No, first we have to catch it.'

'Catch it?' she exclaimed disbelievingly.

He laughed at her expression and said, 'Come and see.'

There was a cluster of boats tied up at the quay and Bruce led the way to one of the larger ones where an elderly native helped Felicity aboard. Bruce jumped lightly down beside her and the fisherman showed them to some cushioned seats in the stern. The throb of the engine seemed noisy at first, but it quietened after they had left the rocky walls of the harbour behind and soon the man was manoeuvring his way deftly through the reefs in the darkness with only a small light to guide him. In the still air the flower scents stole out from the land and Felicity could see the lights of the houses on the waterfront gradually receding as they went further out to sea.

The fisherman said something to Bruce in a language Felicity didn't understand and she looked at him enquiringly.

'It was Creole. Most of the natives speak it and all of the islands have their own form of it in addition to English. On some it's a hackneyed form of French patois, because many of the West Indian islands were owned by the French at some time in their history. Some of the islands have changed hands as many as thirteen times, so theirs is a really polyglot language.' He broke off as the man said something else to him. 'He's going to put on his fishing lamp.'

Despite the warning Felicity found the glare of the bright light hurt her eyes and she put her hand up to shield them.

'Look at the deck,' Bruce told her.

Mystified, Felicity did so, and then gazed in incredulous amazement. She was looking straight down into the depths of the sea where a myriad coloured shoals of fish darted among the glowing orange of the jagged coral reefs. A small octopus scuttled away behind a rock and then a long conger eel swam up to investigate the source of light. Instinctively Felicity flinched away and she felt Bruce's arm warm against her as he put it protectively round her shoulders. Immediately she sat forward again and became very interested in the fish.

'It's a glass-bottomed boat, isn't it? I've read about them, of course, but I had no idea there were any on the islands.'

'They're very useful for night fishing. Watch now,

54

and when a suitable fish comes along old William will hook it out for us.'

Silently they watched until a large grey fish swam slowly into view, then with incredible speed the fisherman had hooked the fish with a long spear and thrown it wriggling frantically into the bottom of the boat. Felicity found that she couldn't look; it was silly, she was a doctor and had seen far worse that very day, but she couldn't look. When she finally turned round she found Bruce watching her with a curious, gentle look in his eyes.

'All over now. I hope you're hungry; that was a big fish.'

'Yes, I am quite. Are we going to take it back to the harbour and have it cooked for us?'

'Why go back to the harbour when we have a perfectly good restaurant right here?' He waved an arm towards the front of the boat and Felicity saw that the old man had uncovered a small stove and was already cooking pieces of the fish in a large stewpan over the glowing heat.

Soon he was placing a small fold-up table in front of them and bringing them plates piled high with cubes of piping-hot fish laid on a bed of peppered rice. Slices of home-baked crusty bread complemented the meal and Felicity found that she didn't mind so much about the fish, after all. Bruce produced a bottle of wine from a plastic bucket filled with ice and poured large glassfuls for all of them. Felicity sipped hers sparingly, but old William took his to the other end of the boat where he helped himself to the rest of the fish and ate and drank liberally.

'Does he speak English?' Felicity asked.

'Not very much. He prefers Creole.' He went on to tell her many other things about the West Indies, and Felicity realised that he had a wide knowledge of his subject and especially of the problems facing its peoples.

After they had finished their al fresco meal, William steered them back safely to the quay and wished them a hearty goodnight. Slowly they drove back through the moonlit night; they didn't talk much, but the silence was not unpleasant or embarrassing as Felicity had expected it to be. Bruce stopped the car a little away from the clinic and came round to open the door for her.

'I thought we could walk the rest of the way. Don't want to wake any of the patients.'

Felicity stepped from the car and raised her head to take in the beauty of the starlit night. 'There are a thousand different scents,' she said with pleasure.

Bruce took her shawl from her. 'You'd better put this on, it can be chilly at night.' The moonlight enhanced the shadows of his face giving him a dark, satanic look and she was suddenly very aware of him standing tall beside her. He put the shawl carefully about her shoulders, lifting her hair gently out of the way. 'I like your hair like that, loose and soft. The way you wear it when you're working makes you look terribly efficient and too much like the archetype of a dedicated career woman.'

They were walking up the road leading to the clinic and Felicity suddenly realised that time was short. If an opportunity was going to arise, it had to be soon.

'I am a dedicated career woman,' she managed to say, while her thoughts ran feverishly on. What could she do? Scream the place down and accuse him of trying to rape her? He would hardly try on the clinic doorstep, she answered herself cynically, and besides, she knew that you needed some evidence of bruising and mistreatment to make a charge like that stick.

He had said something else to her, but she hadn't heard and he had to repeat the question. 'Are you sure that you really want to devote yourself to your work? Doesn't romance come into the picture at all?'

'I'm not the romantic type,' she answered firmly.

'I wonder.' He put his hands on her shoulders and turned her round to face him. For a terrible moment she thought that he was going to try to kiss her and she stiffened with apprehension. Perhaps he sensed it, for he merely said softly, 'Why did you come to Trenaka, Felicity?'

She turned her head away from him and said coldly, 'Because I wanted to travel. It's getting very late, I must ...'

But he had put a hand under her chin and made her lift her head to look at him. 'I have a feeling that you're running away from something—or someone. Is that why you're so against romance?'

Resolutely she pushed herself away from him. 'Really, Mr Gresham, you're becoming ridiculous! My reasons for coming to Trenaka are nothing to do with you,' she lied in her teeth.

He smiled in the half-light. 'Evidently not.' Then he surprised her yet again that night as he raised two fingers to his lips and then gently touched them under her chin. 'Goodnight, Felicity.' And he was gone, stepping briskly away into the darkness.

Felicity went into the clinic, her thoughts in turmoil. Automatically she checked with the night nurse that all was well before going to her own room. Tonight there was no photograph of Peter to give her courage; that was locked away in the drawer of her desk at the MacAllisters' bungalow, and she was left with a feeling of desolation. The evening had been wasted; no opportunity for revenge had even suggested itself to her and she was frustrated by her failure. Sighing, she turned out the light and hoped that somehow, something would present itself before she left Sancreed.

Sister Phillips had spread the word for her and the next afternoon about fifteen native women with babies or young toddlers turned up to hear about the family planning clinic she was hoping to start on the island. Carefully and simply Felicity explained what it was all about, and several of the young mothers decided to take part in the project. It was when she was taking down personal details for the records that Felicity hit the first snag. When asked for their husband's name most of the girls giggled and said that they weren't married. 'I've got a man all right, doctor, but me and him, we aren't married,' one girl in a tight red dress and turban told her, then giggled behind her hand. For a moment Felicity was nonplussed, but decided that if the girls weren't married that they needed help more than ever, and went ahead with her work, making a mental note to ask Sister Phillips about the matter later.

Two more men patients were able to go home that evening, so Felicity volunteered to drive them in the hospital van. A nurse came with her to direct her along the unknown roads which Felicity took slowly and gently, trying hard not to jolt the patients. The men both lived in the small village in which the tree had fallen and she soon saw the grim toll it had taken. Three houses had been completely crushed and two others damaged, but already the debris had been cleared and temporary buildings erected to house the homeless.

A throng of workmen were busy with repair work on the damaged buildings, but many of them rushed over to help the injured men from the van and to welcome them home. The villagers looked curiously at Felicity, not quite sure what to make of her, so to break the ice she bent and talked to some of the children. Soon their mothers joined in and before long she was being taken to see the damage, while they excitedly explained their own parts in the events of the night of the storm.

Bruce had made no contact with her that day and Felicity was beginning to feel afraid that she had offended him by her coldness and that he had decided not to seek her company again. Without really admitting it to herself, she was on the lookout for him, expecting to find him supervising the workers, but it was the resident officer who came over to meet her.

'Brought some of the walking wounded back?' he

greeted her jocularly. 'They'll be the heroes of the hour. Made a bit of a mess, didn't it?' he added with typical British genius for understatement.

'It must have been a big tree,' Felicity agreed.

'An old palm, about fifty feet high. Trouble was it brought some other trees down with it. We've had to saw them up before we could get cracking on the repairs. Bruce Gresham's gone over to one of the larger islands to get a couple of generators so that we can get along quicker.' He went on talking about the work, but Felicity hardly listened, for she had heard the only item of news that really interested her.

She spent the evening writing up the patients' records, deciding that the cases left in her charge were doing so well that it would probably be safe for her to leave Sancreed in two more days, so the next morning she went to the Government Office to talk to Mac on the radio. He told her that the amputee was coming along well and that he would arrange for transport to take her off Sancreed the following day.

On returning to the clinic she had intended to ask Sister Phillips to explain the mystery of all the unmarried mums on the island, but found the nurse in the middle of delivering yet another little islander, so the matter went completely out of her head as she watched the birth— a small miracle that she never tired of.

Doctor and nurse were both laughing at the name that had been chosen for the tiny baby, for his mother had decided to call him Maximilian, when there was a knock at the door of the office. Felicity felt her skin begin to tighten, for she had half been expecting a message from Bruce all morning, but when the Sister called, 'Come in,' Felicity gave an exclamation of pleasure.

'David! What a surprise. What on earth are you doing on Sancreed? I thought you were miles away.'

David grinned. 'Well, I heard you were here and decided that the blight needed to be dealt with right away.'

'Good heavens, am I the blight?' she teased him.

He looked taken aback for a moment. 'I didn't mean ...' He broke off and frowned in mock exasperation. 'I see you haven't changed. Come on, I'm taking you to lunch.'

Felicity didn't wait for further persuasion but ran to take off her white coat and change her sensible shoes for pretty, frivolous sandals. A hasty comb through her loosened hair, fresh lipstick, and she was ready.

'Where are we going?' she asked as she joined him.

'A little restaurant down by the dock. It's owned by a Chinese, an old lascar, who makes a fantastic sweet and sour chicken.'

'Mm, sounds lovely.'

It was odd how at ease she always felt with David; there were none of the tensions and flare-ups that characterized her meetings with Bruce. But then, she thought with irony, David hadn't murdered her brother; she wished him only well, while Bruce Gresham she wished every conceivable ill that she could think of.

The clientele of the Chinese restaurant was a mixture of races, many of them sailors from the banana boats that called at the smaller islands to pick up cargo. From where they sat under a gaily striped umbrella on the dockside, Felicity could see one of these boats being loaded by women carrying bunches of bananas on their heads from the wharf to the iron-jawed hatches that gaped in the side of the ship. The women came at a smooth, noiseless trot, the heavy head-load poised precariously, but only occasionally steadied by a light touch of the fingers. Their faces were thrown forward, chins raised, their eyes intent on their task. Juice from the bananas dripped from the fruit and made dark stains on their dresses from neck to hem.

'They keep that up all day and sometimes through the night until all the cargo is loaded,' David told her, seeing her interest. 'Then the ship masters rig up arc lights which make the whole deck as bright as day. But when the dawn comes the women start to sing that song, "Day, oh, day, oh, day be light and I want to go home".'

His description made Felicity feel infinitely sorry for the hard-working women, so she said somewhat angrily, 'Why don't the men do some of the work?'

'Surely you're not going to deprive the women of their independence?' said a familiar voice, and Felicity jumped as she saw Bruce walking along the quay towards them. 'That's hardly the act of one of our newly liberated career women!' His voice was mocking and there was none of the gentleness of their last meeting about him today.

David pulled out a chair and invited him to join them, taking for granted that Felicity wouldn't object. But she did object, she had been looking forward to a pleasant meal alone with David.

'The work is much too hard for them physically. They must be absolutely exhausted after a few hours of labouring in this heat, especially at the pace they're working at,' she said forcibly.

'They're born to it. If you look you'll see that some of the women are quite young. And they wouldn't thank you if you tried to take their livelihoods away from them—many of them have families to support,' Bruce said callously.

'Why don't their husbands support them?' she pursued. 'I suppose they're just too lazy?'

'Most of them probably aren't married,' Bruce replied, watching her angry expression with an amused curl at the corner of his mouth, while David was openly grinning.

'Oh, as a matter of fact I was going to ask about that.' She explained about the clinic and asked in puzzlement, 'Is it just one of the anthropological traditions of Sancreed?'

Bruce turned to David. 'Perhaps you'd like to explain the situation to Felicity?' he said blandly.

'Oh, no, you're the expert,' David refused hastily.

'Coward!' He turned back to Felicity. 'Well, you'll be pleased to hear that among the natives of the islands there's a mainly matriarchal society. It stems from the times of the large plantation owners when the slaves were segregated, except for mating, of course, and there were no family groups. Now only about one third of the women are legally married, although there are many common law marriages, and these are strongly mother-daughter-granddaughter relationships, with the man's status in the unit depending entirely on what he can provide.' His face completely expressionless, he added, 'I take it you approve of such an arrangement?'

Felicity looked at him suspiciously, not sure whether he was making fun of her, but she was saved from answering by the appearance of the waiter, who came to take their order. After some wrangling as they all liked different things, they settled on a choice of dishes that seemed to cover half the menu, and certainly covered the whole of their table and a heated trolley when it came. Felicity helped herself liberally to the exotic dishes, trying not to think how much nicer it would have been if Bruce hadn't turned up.

It seemed that he had been looking for David and had been told where to find him, for after they had eaten and Felicity had sunk back in her chair feeling sleepy from the wine they had drunk with the meal, Bruce began to ask David about his progress with the blight. Felicity watched them through half-closed lashes; David, so Nordic-looking with his fair hair, open, honest face and ready smile. She felt that one would always know exactly where one stood with David. And Bruce? She turned her head slightly to look at him. David was drawing some sort of diagram on a piece of paper and Bruce was tilting his head to look and listen, his expression inscrutable. Because his attention was not on her she was able to study his features and almost detachedly she decided that he was extremely good-looking with his straight nose and rather long-lashed eyes. She supposed that some women, of whom Diane Cunningham was obviously one, would think him highly eligible. Her gaze dropped to his hands where he pointed out something on the diagram; they were long tapering hands with strong fingers, rather like a surgeon's she had once seen. She could imagine them stroking, caressing ... Suddenly her eyes flew open and she found Bruce looking directly at her. He held her gaze and she felt herself flushing as if he had guessed what she was thinking. Fiercely she tried to tear her eyes away, but his were like steel magnets and she felt as if she were being hypnotised.

She was brought back to earth by David banging his glass on the table; he had been talking away, but had become aware that neither of them were listening to him and so had decided to make his presence felt. Felicity jumped guiltily and went redder than ever, but Bruce merely grinned, and picking up David's diagram said, 'That's an interesting theory, David. I'll bear it in mind,' and rose to leave them.

'By the way,' he added as a parting shot, 'I've been designated to take you back with me to Trenaka tomorrow, Felicity. I'll pick you up at about four o'clock!'

The spray created by the wash made a glistening aureole about the boat as it sped across the undulating sea. Felicity, in suntop and shorts, was thrilled by the speed at which they seemed to travel as she watched the frothing waves disappear underneath the keel.

'Is it a government boat?' she enquired, allowing the breeze to blow her hair into a shimmering cloud about her head.

'No, the *Salamander* belongs to me.' Bruce watched her as, like a child, she leant over the side to trail her fingers in the ocean. 'I bought her when I first came out to Trenaka.'

The boat was smaller than the big hospital launch but

larger than the motor boat that the hospital staff also used for short trips to the nearer islands.

'This type of boat is called a cabin cruiser and can be used for quite long trips,' he told her. 'Come and have a go at steering her.'

'May I really? I've never driven a boat before,' she felt it necessary to warn him.

'Don't worry, I'll watch you. Just hold her steady on the same course that she's on now.'

Rather timidly at first, then with growing confidence she took the wheel and piloted the craft across the seemingly endless ocean.

'It's much better than driving a car,' Felicity confided, her cheeks glowing from the breeze. 'But how do you know which way to go when there aren't any signposts?'

Bruce laughed aloud. 'You landlubber! There are such things as charts. You plot your course and then sail on compass bearings.' He looked down at her golden hair blown into tangles by the wind, then put out a hand to smooth a stray lock that lay across her bare shoulder. 'Perhaps I'll teach you how to sail.'

Felicity froze at his touch and the wheel slipped from her nerveless fingers. It spun wildly and suddenly the boat yawed to starboard and was hit broadside on by a large wave. The boat lurched drunkenly and she lost her footing and would have fallen against the chart table if Bruce hadn't caught and held her. For a moment her nostrils were filled with the oily, tobaccoey scents of his sea sweater, and then she was set firmly down in a corner while he grabbed the wheel and righted the boat.

To her indignation, Felicity saw that he was laughing at her, his eyebrows raised mockingly. With as much dignity as she could muster in the swaying boat, she hauled herself to her feet and walked past him to go down into the cabin. He didn't ask why she had let go of the wheel—he didn't have to. He knew very well that he had only to touch her and she went to pieces. Damn the man, she thought viciously, and slammed the cabin door, determined to stay there till they reached Trenaka.

Gillian Marsh's barbecue party was an informal affair that started on the patio of their house where a steel band alternated with a disco, across the lawn that was being used as a dance floor, and drifted down towards the beach where a fire of driftwood had been lit. Nearly all the Service staff and their wives were there, except Sir Miles and Lady Steventon and David who was still away, so there was a happy relaxed atmosphere at this, the first barbecue party of the summer season. Gillian had really gone to town, with coloured lights and decorative lanterns bobbing about in the trees and hired waiters dressed as slaves. The steaks grilling slowly over the fire smelt delicious; the music, though loud, was catchy, and with Geoff Lord as her escort Felicity was determined to enjoy herself.

Bruce was there with Diane, who looked less harassed away from Cecily Steventon's eagle eye. They had all exchanged greetings earlier, but it was some time later, when Diane was dancing with Colin Marsh, that Bruce came over to Felicity and Geoff.

'May I have this dance, Felicity?' The request was a simple one, but Felicity heard a distinct challenge in his voice. She hadn't seen him since she had bidden him a hasty goodbye on the quay after he had brought her back from Sancreed and he had made no attempt to get in touch with her. She knew that he was expecting her to again make some excuse not to dance with him, probably, and correctly, thinking that she was too afraid of her own reactions to let herself be close to him.

So, with an answering bravado, she gave him an absolutely brilliant smile and said brightly, 'Why, I'd *love* to, Bruce.' Finishing her Planter's Punch at one gulp, she placed the empty glass in Geoff's hand, trying not to see the bemused look on his face, and then swept into Bruce's arms, holding herself quite close to him with her left hand high on his shoulder almost touching the silky hairs at the back of his neck. If her action surprised him he didn't let her see it, merely looking at her quizzically as she chattered vivaciously on about nothing in particular.

'You're very gay tonight?'

Felicity fluttered her eyelashes and smiled sweetly while contriving at the same time to lean rather heavily against him. She was hoping that her performance would make him think her quite unfit to dance and that he would quickly escort her back to Geoff, but instead he took her right hand more firmly in his and tightened his hold on her back so that she was pressed even closer to him. Unmistakably she felt his lips touch her hair and then her ear. She froze rigid and missed her footing. He was holding her so close that the stumble was hardly noticed, but she was still standing rigidly and wouldn't move.

Bruce looked down at her, his eyes full of mock surprise, 'Darling, why stop when this dance was becoming so interesting?' He tried to pull her into the rhythm again, but Felicity put her left hand against his chest and tried unsuccessfully to push him away.

'Let me go!' she hissed at him.

He was deliberately obtuse. 'But isn't this what you wanted?'

'I didn't mean it, you *know* I didn't!' Her cheeks were flushed with embarrassment and indignation as she realised that other dancers were beginning to look at them curiously as they stood still in the middle of the floor.

'Do I?' Still he wouldn't let her go. He looked down at her for a long moment and then abruptly loosened his hold. 'Haven't you yet learned that if you play with fire you'll get hurt? Now let's start all over again, shall we?' he said coldly. 'May I have this dance, Felicity?'

She would have given anything in the world to have said, 'No', but she was suddenly afraid, and so, without looking at him, she said in a small voice, 'Yes, please.'

Bruce took her in his arms again but this time held her

loosely, at a comfortable distance away from him. The tune was a slow one and to Felicity it seemed to drag on for ever. He guided her carefully among the other dancers, but she kept her gaze fixedly on the buttonhole in his lapel which was at her eye-level, and concentrated on trying to still the nervous shivers that ran through her despite the hot night.

When the music at last stopped he escorted her to a chair, said formally, 'Thank you so much,' and walked away without a backward glance to where Diane was watching them with a puzzled frown. Felicity immediately whisked herself to the bathroom where she leant against the cool tiled wall and felt physically ill. Slowly she bathed her temples and stared at her pale face in the mirror. What she had done, she realised now, had been extremely foolish; men like Bruce Gresham would know women too well to be taken in by such a silly ploy as hers had been. Well, he had called her bluff and she had lost, been beaten to the ground.

To add to the misery of the evening, when she went to find Geoff to take her home he was missing from the crowd of guests. She found him eventually in the darkened shrubbery. He was thanking his hostess for the party in a most personal manner! Hastily Felicity retreated and went to tell Ellen that she had a headache and would drive herself home. Let everyone think what they liked, she just couldn't stay there any longer; she felt too humiliated.

Hopelessly she climbed into bed and buried her face in the pillow; it seemed that she would never be able to defeat this man who was so in control of himself and of every situation!

CHAPTER FOUR

TIME began to pass quickly on Trenaka as Mac allowed Felicity to visit neighbouring islands to set up her clinics and to give child welfare classes for the native women. Usually she travelled in the small motor boat with Joey for a pilot and with his younger brother, Daniel, coming along for the ride. Felicity very soon persuaded Joey to teach her how to pilot the boat, and, as he was immensely proud of his seamanship, he was only too pleased to show off to the lady doctor. She was a quick learner and had picked up the rudiments of navigation well enough to steer by chart and compass, but always handed over to Joey when leaving or entering Trenaka harbour; his self-esteem wouldn't allow him to be seen being piloted by a woman.

Spring was giving way to summer now and Felicity's tan was becoming a deeper gold, but she decided that her back was lighter than her front, so, one Sunday, while the servants had their day off and the MacAllisters had gone to visit friends on another island for the weekend, Felicity took a gaily striped towel down to the beach below the bungalow, and dressed only in a pale blue bikini, settled down with a book to the serious business of getting an even sun-tan. She was just beginning to feel that perhaps she had had enough when she heard someone approaching and looked up to see Bruce, in shirt and shorts, walking over the sand towards her.

'Good morning. Mind if I join you?' Without waiting for an answer he dropped easily to the ground beside her.

'Please do,' Felicity said with irony, and rolled over so

that she had her back to him as she reached for the blue cotton shirt she had brought with her.

'Let me,' he said politely, and taking the shirt from her held it for her to put on. She had, perforce, to let him help her, but as she buttoned up the shirt she felt it necessary to say, 'Thank you, but I could have managed.'

He looked at her searchingly and she hastily took cover behind her dark glasses. He smiled. 'I know, you think you're a very liberated young lady and that everything a man can do you can do equally well, if not better.' Holding up a hand, he stopped her as she was about to reply. 'Oh, I know you're going to say your work is as good as any man's, but you don't have to; I already know it. But why cut men out of your life completely? They do have their uses sometimes, you know.'

Ignoring the last remark, Felicity said tightly, 'I don't cut men out of my life.'

'No? That must mean that you've let a man into your life before.' His voice was gentle again now. 'And I think that this man must have hurt you in some way—hurt you very much. And that's why you ran away to Trenaka, isn't it?'

Felicity stared at him wordlessly; he was so wrong, so very wrong—and yet so right. She looked down and concentrated intently on picking up the fine white sand and watching it trickle through her fingers.

'Work isn't everything, Felicity,' he continued. 'It can be a great panacea, but a time will come when it won't be enough.'

'Really?' Her amber eyes flashed at him. 'That hardly seems the right sermon for you to preach this Sunday. From what I've heard since I came here, your ambition knows no limits. Everyone who has mentioned you has always described you as a man whose life is completely given over to his work, never allowing anything to stand in his way—in the way of a future ambassadorship—and even moulding your social life to ...' She broke off abruptly, conscious that her indignant tongue was running away with her.

Bruce looked at her with a frown for a few moments, then seemed to come to a decision, for he got lightly to his feet and reached down to pull her up beside him. 'Go and get some clothes on. Shorts or slacks will do. There's something I want to show you.'

Felicity started to protest, but he picked up her things and hurried her towards the garden.

'I'll go and get the car.' He walked quickly off towards his own house while Felicity went in to change out of her bikini. She kept the blue blouse but added white cotton slacks, rope sandals and a floppy-brimmed straw hat. Curiously she wondered what it was that Bruce was going to show her; evidently it was her outburst about his ruthlessness that had made him decide to take her. Was she, perhaps, going to see another facet of Bruce Gresham, and would it be one she could use for her own purposes?

He was back within ten minutes, but Felicity deliberately kept him waiting while she checked that the bungalow was securely locked before strolling casually down the drive to join him. He said nothing; merely starting up the car and driving towards the southern end of the island. Although it was Sunday there were lots of people working in the fields, many of them women and children.

'Why are they working today?' Felicity asked, confident that Bruce knew all there was to know of the islanders.

'They're planting crops. Those people are mostly descendants of labourers who were brought here from India to work the plantations after the slaves were given their freedom. They are called East Indians in the islands. The whole family from the grandparents down come out to work in the fields at planting time.'

Felicity looked at the children with their large dark eyes, the girls with pigtails of long black hair carefully combed and plaited and glossy with coconut oil. Some of

70

the children were quite tiny, not more than six or seven years old.

'Isn't there a law against such young children being made to work?'

'It only happens occasionally. They're at school during the week.'

The road was beginning to climb now. They drove through a pass between the foothills of the mountains. Shaded by the joined branches of trees edging the road, it gave the effect of travelling through a green tunnel with occasional shafts of light where the sun tried to pierce the roof of branches. A mile or so further on Bruce turned off the main road on to an unmade-up track that wound higher among the hills. They came to a clearing where the track petered out and Bruce said, 'This is where we go on foot. It's only a short way.'

Felicity looked around her but could see nothing out of the ordinary.

'This way.' He led her along a tree-lined path, carefully holding the branches out of the way for her. Then they came to a piece of open land and Felicity gave a gasp of amazement. They were standing on a partially cleared piece of ground of about an acre that was set into a plateau on the side of a steep hill, and all about her for as far as she could see there were panoramic views of the mountains and valleys, and far away a glimpse of the surging ocean.

'It's breathtaking!' she exclaimed. 'Like being an eagle in an eyrie!'

'How do you think a house would look here?'

'Just marvellous,' she said with enthusiasm. 'A low sprawling house with lots of huge picture windows so that you could have this wonderful view from every room.' She drank in the vista for a while longer and then turned to him, unable to contain her curiosity any further. 'Why did you bring me here? I mean, the view is absolutely fantastic—but there was more than that, wasn't there?'

He drew her to a felled tree trunk and they sat down facing the valley.

'Yes, there was. You accused me of having nothing else in life except my work. Well, I have this.'

'You mean it belongs to you?'

'Yes, I discovered it quite by accident and bought it immediately. Whenever I have some free time or feel like getting away, I can come up here and clear some of the land ready for building.'

Felicity looked at him uncertainly. 'You intend to develop the site?'

'I intend to build a house here, yes.'

'So that you can sell it for a profit?' she said dryly.

'What incredible ideas you have about me! No, I intend to build the house for myself, as an escape from the heat of the plain and also from the traumas of the Service.'

'But I thought that . . .'

'I told you,' he interrupted her brusquely, 'you have some utterly incredible ideas about me. Okay, I love my work and I want to get to the top. Is there any crime in that? But I'm just like any other chap; I want a wife and family and a home to come back to. It might not always be here, it could be anywhere in the world that I'm sent to, but I need those things as much as any man. So just try and remember that, will you, the next time you listen to gossip?'

Felicity felt her cheeks reddening. So Bruce was going to build a house so that he could marry Diane. A hilltop hideaway; a love nest instead of an eagle's nest! She had never thought of him as ever being lonely, he had always seemed too self-possessed and confident for that. 'I'm sorry. I jumped to conclusions,' she said in a low voice.

'We all make mistakes.' Sensing her confusion, he went on, 'I've always liked mountains ever since I was taken to Switzerland for a holiday as a kid. After that I made several climbing trips when I was at university, but then

72

my father died and I had to spend my holidays at home with my mother and sister.'

'Home?' Felicity felt as if the question was being dragged out of her.

'A place called Alnswick, in Wiltshire. Do you know it?'

Felicity shook her head, thankful for the floppy brim of her hat that shaded her eyes. 'Do your mother and sister still live there?' she asked as casually as she could.

'My mother does, but my sister, Camilla, lives just outside London. She's married to an architect and has a couple of fine kids.'

'You'll have to get your brother-in-law to design your house for you. What style have you in mind?'

He began to describe his ideas enthusiastically, scratching a plan on a piece of dry earth with a stick, but Felicity wasn't listening. So his sister was happy, with a husband who loved her and two children to mother. Her hands clenched involuntarily. But it was Peter she should have been married to; Peter who had loved his sister first. But Peter was dead; burnt alive in a car crash because of what this man had done to him!

Abruptly she stood up. 'When do you start building?'

Languidly he rose to join her. 'Pretty soon, I think.'

'What do David and Diane think of the site?'

He raised a quizzical eyebrow. 'I don't know. I haven't shown it to anyone else yet,' he said steadily, his grey eyes watching her reaction.

'Then I'm honoured.' She managed to make her voice light. 'Or am I the only one who has accused you of being ruthlessly ambitious before?'

'You're certainly that!' Taking her arm, he led her back to the car and drove to Trenaka town where he insisted she join him for lunch in a small, cool restaurant.

Afterwards he said, 'Would you like to practise your skin-diving this afternoon, or perhaps take my boat out for a sailing lesson?'

Felicity decided that a morning spent in his company

was enough. 'No, thank you. I have something planned for this afternoon.'

'Sure you won't be lonely or bored with the Macs away?'

'Fortunately I can be quite contented in my own company, thank you,' she said rather tartly.

'Ah, yes, I'd forgotten that you're emancipated.' His words were spoken in his usual mocking tones, but his smile robbed them of any malice.

He dropped her at the bungalow but didn't go on to his own house, instead he drove off in the direction of the hills again. Felicity wondered if he was going to clear some more of his land; she gazed after him for a while, then shrugged her shoulders and walked up to the bungalow.

The social life among the European residents increased with the summer. Beach parties were popular and the MacAllisters gave their promised barbecue party which Felicity thoroughly enjoyed, not only for the party itself, but also for the fun she had in helping Ellen to prepare for it. David came back from his 'blight-blasting' trip, as he described it, and again took her diving, although by now she was proficient enough to need only practice and not tuition. This was somewhat curtailed, however, because the cricket season was upon them and David, Bruce, Mac, and Geoff were all in the Service eleven that had a busy programme of fixtures with the local native teams.

At several of the parties Felicity was not alone in noticing that Bruce no longer seemed to act as Diane's escort, as he often came and left alone, or with other bachelors. He would dance with Diane, as he danced with Felicity (who was extremely careful to act very correctly whenever he did so) and also several of the other women, without showing any preference. Once when David was away he took Felicity home from a party, and again pressed his fingers to his lips and placed them under her chin in the unusual gesture only he had.

Gillian pronounced herself bored with cricket and persuaded Felicity to accompany her on a picnic one Sunday instead of watching the match.

'I can't stand another afternoon either making small talk to the wives one sees every day of the week, or else being stuck in the pavilion making endless sandwiches for men who've been standing round in a field all day, watching one man throwing a ball at three bits of wood while another man tries to hit it with a bigger piece of wood!'

Felicity had to laugh at her description of the game but quite sympathised with her; until Mac had taken the trouble to explain the finer points to her, she, too, had found the game rather monotonous, but now she was becoming quite a keen supporter.

Gillian drove to a quiet, deserted beach where they left the car. Then she took Felicity inland again along a neglected, overgrown path that led to an old ruined plantation house. The great house had been built like a fortress for fear of slave uprisings, but now the shutters hung crookedly from their hinges and lizards scuttled among the huge rusted cannon set into concrete bastions on the terrace overlooking the sea.

'I often come here,' Gillian told her. 'It's spooky, but you can imagine the sort of life that was lived here. The people really knew how to live then.'

As they walked back to the beach for their swim before lunch, Felicity wondered if Gillian ever met Geoff here, but then dismissed the thought from her mind. It was really none of her business.

'How are you settling into Trenaka now that you've been here a while?' Gillian asked with deceptive casualness. 'You've certainly managed to create quite a stir. The wives haven't had such a good bit of gossip to discuss over the tea-cups for months.'

Felicity looked at her in bewilderment, halting in her task of unpacking the picnic hamper while Gillian lay back on her beach mat in the sun, smoking a cigarette. 'Created a stir? What do you mean?'

'Oh, come on, my sweet. You don't have to pretend to me. The whole of Trenaka is wondering why Mr Bruce Gresham, that most eligible of bachelors, is no longer escorting the highly suitable, but slightly past it, Miss Diane Cunningham, to the gay social scene. Speculation, to put it mildly, is rife! Have the perfectly matched pair had a row? Impossible; Diane never dared to disagree with anyone in her life. Has Diane found someone else? Hardly, or we would all have known about it. And anyway, there's no one else to find. But has Bruce found someone else? Now there we have a distinct possibility in the glamorous shape of Dr Felicity Lambert, do we not?' she finished, looking hard at her victim.

Felicity stared at her speechlessly for a moment and then, despite herself, began to laugh. That there was a slight note of hysteria it was lost on Gillian, who was completely taken aback by the younger girl's reaction.

'You mean you haven't been out to get him?' she said, her voice less goading than it had been previously.

Shaking her head decisively, Felicity said firmly, 'You must be crazy if you think that. Why, he's the last man ... I'm quite happy with my job and going out with the crowd, thanks very much.'

Gillian frowned in perplexity. 'Then I wonder why ...? Well, anyway, you've been warned, sweetie. Don't be surprised if you get some cool looks from Lady Steventon's set; they all think that you're out to catch Bruce.'

'For heaven's sake,' Felicity remonstrated, 'let's eat our lunch and talk of something else.'

They ate, dozed and swam again before packing up their things to go home.

'Did the pills I prescribed for you help at all?' Felicity

asked casually as she stowed the hamper in the boot of Gillian's car.

'Sure, they were fine. I got Geoff to dish some more out to me.'

Gillian certainly seemed less tense and Felicity could only hope that her affair with Geoff would run its course and eventually end, as end it must, without causing a scandal and hurting Colin.

Felicity thought nothing more of Gillian's warning, putting it down to boredom and an over-fertile imagination, so she was surprised and not displeased a week or so later to receive an invitation to afternoon tea with Lady Steventon.

'She usually invites the women after they've had time to settle in,' Ellen told her when shown the invitation. 'Don't be surprised if she probes into your background. She likes to know if you're her social equal.'

'And likes it even more if she finds you're not!' Mac added irrepressively. He winked at Felicity as Ellen told him off and Felicity grinned back. She knew that they were both eagerly looking forward to the return of their sons for the summer vacation.

'It's not only the hurricane season in the West Indies we're expecting, but the hurricane season in the house too, ye ken, when those two great lads are here,' Ellen had said to her happily.

Feeling cool and composed in a crisp apple-green linen suit, Felicity drove herself to the Residency on the appointed day and was conducted by an austere butler to Lady Steventon's sitting-room at the rear of the building.

'Do come in, Dr Lambert,' her hostess greeted her. 'I thought we would have tea in here rather than the drawing-room, as there are just the two of us.'

Fleetingly Felicity wondered why Diane wasn't joining them, but was soon too busy parrying the older woman's questions to think about it further.

'My husband tells me that the clinics you are setting up have got off to a very successful start. Did you have much experience of this type of work in England?'

'Yes, when I was in general practice and also during my final year in a hospital.'

'You must find working in the West Indies vastly different?'

'But also very stimulating,' Felicity added without going into details.

'It must have been a wrench for you to leave England, although you're an orphan, I believe. Didn't you have any—attachments in England?' Lady Steventon's well-bred face gave nothing away, but Felicity sensed that what had gone before was merely a preamble to the last question.

'Attachments?' she queried, being deliberately vague.

'I meant, wasn't there any young man that you were reluctant to leave behind?'

'No, Lady Steventon, there was not,' Felicity replied bluntly.

'Well, I expect there will be many opportunities for you to meet young men of a suitable background while you're here. David Cameron, for instance; I believe someone told me that you had become quite friendly with him.'

'He was kind enough to teach me to skin-dive, yes.'

'Such a very nice person. I've always liked him ever since he was posted here.'

'Really?' Felicity said unhelpfully, wondering just what this was leading to.

Lady Steventon decided to try another tactic. 'I often arrange little parties among the younger people for Diane. She's my cousin as well as my secretary, you know. You and David must come and make up a four for tennis. She and Bruce play so often together that it will do them good to have some opposition.' She spoke as if the two names were already permanently joined. 'Bruce, of course, is destined for great things in the Service, the very highest positions, and with Diane beside him he will obtain those objectives as a comparatively young man. It is always *so* important for a man to have the right sort of wife, don't you think, Dr Lambert? One who is prepared to give up all her own interests, everything, for his sake and to dedicate herself completely to furthering his career.'

So this is what the invitation was for, Felicity thought. To stop me getting any ideas above my station, any ideas of interfering between Bruce and Diane. My God, if she only knew! Suddenly she felt coldly angry at Lady Steventon's high-handed interference, so she slowly helped herself to a tiny iced cake from the Rockingham china plate before replying, 'I'm afraid I've been much too busy with my own career to give much thought to the qualities needed by the wife of a government official, but after all they're only wives, aren't they? They have no official status.'

Deliberately she made her tone rather cutting and for a moment the other woman's poise slipped a little as she looked at Felicity, her eyebrows raised. Then she nodded her elegant head. 'I'm glad that your work is your first interest, Dr Lambert. If you keep to that principle you should go far.'

Lady Steventon then skilfully changed the subject and the conversation became light and conventional. At five o'clock precisely she rose to signify that the visit was over, and herself saw Felicity out to the white-columned portico where she cordially wished her goodbye. 'Perhaps I may pay a visit to one of your welfare classes, Dr Lambert—or even send Diane as my deputy; it's time she took over some of my duties. I'll arrange a date so that you can have everything properly prepared for her visit.'

Felicity smiled, realising that the Governor's wife had succeeded in putting her firmly in her place, which was well down the ladder below herself and Diane. But as she got in the car and drove slowly home, she wondered whether Diane and Bruce were to be engaged soon. As yet there had been absolutely no opportunity of taking her revenge on Bruce, but she must find a way soon, before any engagement was announced, because she had no wish to hurt Diane along with him. She had nothing against the older girl and, in fact, on the few occasions that they had come in contact, had found herself quite liking her. Exasperatedly she sighed; if only an opportunity would present itself!

'Oh, well played!' an enthusiastic supporter in the crowd applauded as the West Indian batsman hit a useful four.

This Sunday's match was a big event in the cricketing calendar, an 'at home' for the Service side against the first Trenaka eleven, and was being held on the pitch just outside the grounds of the Residency. Bruce was bowling; fast, spinning balls that kept the batsmen on their toes, and the match was becoming quite exciting as the two sides were evenly matched. Mac was the wicket-keeper, almost unrecognisable under all his padding, and Geoff a close-in fielder.

Felicity was officially supposed to be helping Ellen and some of the others of the wives to prepare the teas, but she couldn't resist popping out on to the veranda of the pavilion every now and again to see how the game was progressing.

'Dr Lambert, Dr Lambert!' An urgent voice from the crowd in front of the railing diverted her attention from Bruce's next run up. She saw the features of Joey's brother, Daniel, looking up at her. 'A message has come over the radio to the hospital, doctor. They need a doctor over on Fortuna. Someone is very sick.'

Felicity gave a sigh of disappointment as she realised that she was going to miss the end of the match, but then smiled at Daniel and told him to wait by her Mini. Going into the pavilion she sought out Ellen and told her she was answering an emergency.

'That's the penalty for being on call,' Ellen laughed

at her. 'Shall I send a message out to Mac on the field?'

'No, that won't be necessary,' Felicity assured her. 'I'd hate to disturb him in the middle of the most important game of the season.'

When they arrived at the quayside, Daniel jumped down into the motor boat and began to prepare to put to sea.

'Where's Joey?' Felicity asked him.

'He's back at the cricket match, Dr Lambert. He said I'm grown up enough to take you now,' Daniel added proudly, throwing out his skinny chest.

'Did he?' Felicity said disbelievingly. 'You mean he didn't want to miss the match, don't you?' Daniel grinned impishly and Felicity found it was impossible to be cross with him. 'Okay, Daniel, let's go. You're the captain today.'

Despite being only fifteen years old, Daniel was, she knew, an experienced sailor, having taken her to Fortuna, a very small island only about fifteen miles from Trenaka, several times before. And even if she had had any doubts about his capabilities, she had none about her own ability to handle the motor boat.

Their journey to Fortuna was uneventful and Felicity was soon examining her patient. This was a little girl, the daughter of a young American couple who had bought a small hotel on Fortuna only two years before. The parents were waiting anxiously outside the building that served as a clinic on the island while the resident nurse helped Felicity.

'When was she brought in, nurse?'

'Just before we radioed. I figured she needed help pretty badly.'

'You were right. I'm afraid the appendix is very badly inflamed and we'll have to operate as soon as I can get her back to Trenaka.'

Quickly she informed the parents and arranged for someone to send a message ahead to the hospital. The mother, Mrs Anderson, decided to accompany them back to Trenaka and soon, without waiting for a reply to their message, they began the return journey with the girl, Tracey, safely bedded down in the bunk in the tiny cabin, with her mother beside her.

Felicity went up to stand beside Daniel at the wheel and was surprised to feel how the wind had strengthened. Taking a silk head square from her bag she tied it securely round her hair to stop it flying into her eyes. The blue sky was streaked with thin streamers of cloud and the sea, usually an unruffled blue-green, was broken by white wave crests whipped up by the wind. Below the waves the sea was heaving rhythmically with a bigger swell than she had ever noticed before.

'Is it a storm coming?' She almost had to shout to make herself heard above the wind.

Daniel nodded, 'I guess so, doctor.'

'How bad?'

'Don't you worry, miss. We'll be back in port before she breaks.'

'Daniel, did you check the weather forecast before we left?' she demanded anxiously.

The boy looked away, but Felicity caught his shoulders and made him face her. He didn't answer and looked sheepishly at the deck.

'You didn't check it, did you?'

'No, Dr Lambert, I guess I forgot.'

'Then you'd just better give it full throttle and hope that we get back before the storm breaks.' Going back into the cabin, she checked on her patient and talked with Mrs Anderson, a girl not much older than herself, with a likeable, open nature. Suddenly Felicity lifted her head to listen to the noise of the engine. It had altered from its usual well-oiled purring sound and had begun to miss and splutter. Hastily she ran on deck and found a worried-looking Daniel.

'What's happened?'

'I'm not sure, miss. Sounds like maybe the jets are

blocked.' Even as he spoke the engine coughed and died.

'You go and look at the engine while I hold her steady.'

The wind was a high-pitched whine now and as the boat wallowed in the waves Felicity soon became wet with the spray. There were oilskins in one of the cabin lockers, she knew, but she was afraid to leave the wheel to find them. After what seemed ages Daniel came back on deck, his hands smothered in grease which he wiped off on his jeans.

'I'm sorry, doctor. The thing has seized up solid and I don't know how to repair it.'

'But, Daniel, we've got to get the child to hospital immediately!' But the youngster wasn't listening; he was hastily looking round at the darkening sky and then down at the compass. Felicity followed his gaze and to her horror saw the needle jumping wildly in its glass case.

'What is it? An electric storm ...' She broke off as she saw his eyes big with fear.

'No, miss. This is a hurricane!'

He had not shouted the words, in fact he had spoken little above a whisper, but Felicity had heard them as clearly as if they had been shouted through a megaphone. For a few seconds her brain refused to function and then, desperately, she tried to remember what little she knew of hurricanes. The season, she recalled, was from July to October, but this was only the beginning of July; perhaps the boy had made a mistake and this was just a storm, but looking at him she knew he had not. He had lived through too many of them to be mistaken now.

'We must send up a distress signal,' she said practically. 'How many have we?'

They found two packets of flares, four in each packet. 'Send one up now and then another in twenty minutes,' she told him.

The little boat was so low in the water that their horizon was limited, but she hoped that one of the many ships that plied between the islands might be in the vicinity. Daniel set off the first rocket and they watched it climb high into the threatening sky before bursting into a bright ball of orange flame. Felicity sent the boy down to try the engine again and then grimly went to tell Mrs Anderson what had happened, but found Tracey being violently sick. The boat was rocking and rolling in the waves despite Felicity's having lashed the wheel, and although Mrs Anderson was doing her best to take care of Tracey, she looked as if she, too, might be ill at any moment. Felicity made her swallow some anti-seasickness tablets and insisted that she lie on the other bunk. On gently examining the child's distended abdomen again, Felicity began to feel really worried. The vomiting had not helped at all and she wished with all her heart that there had been a radio on the motor boat. She did her best for her patient and then put on oilskins before going back on deck to make sure Daniel sent the second flare.

'Any sign of a ship?' She had to really shout now against the screaming wind.

Daniel shook his head and put on the oilskins she had brought him while Felicity held the wheel in an almost useless attempt to keep the boat into the wind. The boy sent off the flare and they eagerly scanned the sky for an answering light, but it remained as black and lowering as ever.

Taking the bailer, Daniel began to try and empty out some of the water that had collected in the well of the boat, but as fast as he emptied it overboard another wave would smash against the side and pour spray over them. Felicity forced herself to wait a further twenty minutes before sending off the third rocket, although the temptation to send them up one after the other was almost irresistible. Gracefully it climbed, its vapour trail lost in the clouds, then exploded just like any Guy Fawkes Night firework. Desperately they searched the skies, and then both shouted with excitement; far over to starboard an answering light had split the darkness.

Quickly Felicity turned the boat and tried to let it drift in the direction of the light. They had to send up another two rockets before the other boat came in sight, and to Felicity's surprise she recognised the hospital launch. Expertly it was brought alongside and a rope thrown to be made fast. A man in oilskins climbed precariously down from the launch, and carefully timing his moment, jumped on to the heaving deck of the smaller craft. For a second Felicity was held tightly against him as he steadied himself, and she said laughingly, 'Am I glad to see you!'

'Are you, Felicity?' The voice was warm and without mockery, but she knew it immediately.

'Bruce!' she exclaimed in amazement. 'I expected Geoff or Mac.'

'They're both needed at the hospital. We get quite a few casualties during a hurricane. But let's get you and your patient aboard the launch.'

Soon they were safely aboard the hospital ship with the motor boat in tow behind and heading back to Trenaka.

A worried Felicity sought Bruce out on the bridge. 'I'm afraid my patient is very ill. If she isn't operated on immediately the appendix will rupture and I might not be able to save her.'

'Can you do the operation yourself?'

'Yes, but not on this boat; it's much too unsteady. Is there an island nearer than Trenaka where we can go ashore? I've everything I need on the launch and it can be carried ashore quite quickly.'

Bruce looked at her, his forehead creased in a frown, his mouth grim. Turning to Joey, who was at the helm, he said, 'That old key the pirates used is about a mile from here, isn't it?' Quickly he studied the chart and then gave a new heading.

Travelling as fast as they dared through the storm, the key soon came in sight and Bruce himself took the helm to steer the boat along a channel of close-packed coral heads guarding the entrance to a lagoon. He brought the boat in at a fair rate, then, when it looked as if he was going to crash on the reef, he twisted the wheel, the boat spun on her tail, he cut the motor and the launch sidled neatly into sheltered water. The tiny island curved in a horseshoe shape round the lagoon, enclosing it to west, north and east; and to the south an old ruined fort commanded the channel to the deep sea beyond. It was no wonder that the place had been used in the past by pirates, Felicity thought as she gazed around her. It was a perfect hiding place.

Caves honeycombed the slope from the foot to the crest of the hill and it was one of these that Bruce suggested she use to perform the operation.

'What about the fort?' They were sheltered now from the full force of the wind and she didn't have to shout so much.

'No good, I'm afraid. The roof fell in and it's open to the elements. But there's a big cave that I think will do.'

Quickly she pointed out the items of equipment that she would need and Bruce and the crew members began to carry them ashore. The entrance to the cave was some way up the slope and as Felicity climbed the path towards it she felt her legs sting as the gusting wind scooped up the sharp sand in fierce flurries. The cave was entered by a short tunnel with the main chamber off to the right. It was roughly circular in shape, about thirty feet across and twenty feet high in the middle. As an operating theatre it left much to be desired, but it would have to do.

Felicity quickly prepared her makeshift theatre with the table and trolley they had brought from the launch and arranged her equipment. There was an encouraging smile for Tracey and her mother, but it was Bruce that she turned to for assistance when she needed it, for Mrs Anderson was too seasick and anxious to be of any real help. Calmly, and as quickly as she could, Felicity anaesthetised the child and began the operation, worried that the appendix might already have ruptured. But she was in time, and she worked, skilfully and unhurriedly now, cutting and stitching as Bruce held a ship's lantern steady for her; a light that never wavered. Eventually the job was done to her satisfaction and she tied the last stitch and dressed the wound. The child was breathing quietly and easily. At last Felicity relaxed, aware of being extremely tired.

She gave Mrs Anderson a weary smile. 'Tracey will sleep for a while longer, but you can come and sit by her if you like.'

The young mother needed no second bidding and hurried to her daughter's side where she picked up the limp little hand and held it against her cheek, tears running unashamedly down her face. Hastily Felicity turned away, feeling a lump in her own throat. Taking off her surgical clothes, she walked down the short tunnel to the entrance of the cave, unaware that Bruce was watching her.

Rain was slanting down out of the black scudding clouds, pitting the foam-streaked waters of the bay. The noise of the hurricane was immense and primitive; the roar of the wind, the spit and splash of the rain as it poured down out of the savage sky, and the distant thunder of the sea breaking on the cliffs and over the reef and then rushing across the lagoon to assault the beach with torrents of foam and spray.

The force and rage of the hurricane was so strange and new that she was fascinated by it and for a while was not aware that Bruce had come to stand beside her. He tried to say something to her, but she couldn't hear and shook her head. He put his hands on her shoulders and drew her close to say it in her ear, but still she couldn't understand and shrugged helplessly.

He looked down at her, his eyes intent, the mocking smile gone from his mouth. Slowly he lowered his head and sought her lips with his. At first he was gentle, then he held her closer to him as the kiss deepened. Felicity felt helpless in his arms, as if the storm had drained all the strength and fight from her. She felt as if she had been sucked into the vortex of the hurricane, and suddenly knew that this had been inevitable from the start. Fate had brought this to pass and she surrendered to it as she surrendered her lips to the bruising passion of his kiss.

Slowly, reluctantly, he released her at last and as her eyes stared into his, Felicity became aware of the silence all around them. The wind and sea were no longer screaming furies; all was still, but there was no sun, no singing of sea birds; it was stifling, ominous quiet.

'What is it? Is the hurricane over?' She felt bemused, lost.

'No,' he spoke softly, but his voice was loud in the echoing silence. 'It's only half over. We're in the eye of the hurricane. The worst is yet to come.'

Yes, Felicity realised, for him the worst was still to come. For she had suddenly seen her way clear before her. If she could make Bruce fall in love with her, get him completely within her power, and then hurt him as he had hurt her, it would be an even more satisfying vengeance than she could possibly have hoped for.

CHAPTER FIVE

DIMLY in the distance Felicity heard a telephone ringing and tried to force herself into wakefulness. Was she 'on call' and ought she to answer it? She tried to remember, but everything seemed very vague in her mind. Besides, the ringing had stopped and she turned lazily over to go back to sleep, but she slowly realised that sunlight was glinting between the slats of the venetian blinds. Daytime? Why was she in bed during the day? Then with startling clearness the events of the previous day came rushing back to her. The hurricane! It was like trying to remember a nightmare; it was there, frightening, terrifying, but detail receded with each moment of wakefulness.

They had all had to spend the entire night in the cave; Daniel, Joey and the crew, Mrs Anderson and Tracey, herself and Bruce. There had been no more opportunities for private talk between them after that unforgettable, horrible kiss, for Joey had called to say that Tracey was stirring and Felicity had hurried thankfully back to her patient and remained at her side throughout the night.

When dawn came the surrounding sea was smooth as glass, but the surface moved in slow undulations, recalling the storm that had been. The sky was grey-blue and cloudless but for a few cotton-wool puffs low in the north. In the east pink and orange hues tinged the sky as the sun climbed towards the horizon. The lagoon was flat calm now, the water still muddied by the stirring of the hurricane. Above the eastern horizon the sky became livid with new colour. As Felicity watched, a bank of dense purple shaded into ruby red, then cerise, then orange and yellow against a sky lightening from grey to pale blue. Long shimmering beams radiated from the edge of the sea, to fade and die as the lip of the sun rose into view.

Everywhere there was an impression of dampness soon to be evaporated by the returning day. The trees and rocks, the sand and the water picked up colour from the sun. The whole island seemed warm and alive again. Ducks were winging back and soon all the birds would come; the boobies, the flamingoes and the pelicans, from where they had waited in some secret sanctuary until the hurricane was over.

The equipment had been reloaded on the launch and they had all, Tracey included, breakfasted on the way back to Trenaka. Ellen and Mac had been awaiting them on the quayside and after warm, relieved hugs from them both, Mac had taken charge of Mrs Anderson and Tracey, while Ellen whisked Felicity home and listened to her story while she bathed, then insisted she go straight to bed.

Now, looking at her wrist-watch, she saw that it was early evening, but still she didn't try to get up. Vaguely she wondered if Bruce, too, had gone home to bed. Somehow she thought not; he appeared to be the type who could take a night spent in a cave in the middle of a hurricane in his stride. Reluctantly she turned her mind back to the incident during the eye of the storm. Was it merely because his deep male instincts had been roused by the utter primevalness of the hurricane? Instincts that he normally had under full control beneath his urbane, charming manner? No, his self-possessedness would never allow him to act against his will, she admitted reluctantly.

Slowly she got out of bed and sat in front of the dressing table mirror to brush her hair. But the brush remained inert in her hand. Her reflection stared back at her; the golden aureole of tousled curls, the large amber eyes with sooty shadows of fatigue enhancing their brilliance, her mouth, unmade-up and sensuous in her tanned skin.

Bruce Gresham had kissed that mouth for the simple reason that he had wanted to. Because he wanted her. The kiss had told her so, and she knew that soon he would come to claim her, to demand from her what her responding kiss had promised!

Shivering uncontrollably, she let the brush fall from her slack fingers and put her head in her hands. Was this then to be her destiny—that she should have to sacrifice herself to her enemy, a man she loathed, so that she could bring about his ruin? Desperately she tried to think of some alternative, but she had thought and thought it over a thousand times before; there seemed to be no other way than to make him fall in love with her.

Abruptly she rose and went into the bathroom to shower, first hot, then cold, three times over. Felicity began to feel better, less defeated. Well, if he offered her a closer relationship she would have to accept it; there was no way out of it. At least, she thought cynically, as his mistress she would have a double weapon with which to wreck his career. Though how he would keep the affair from Diane, she failed to see. One thing was sure, he would never let it come between his career and his marriage to Diane; which, when you came to think of it, was only part of his career anyway. Perhaps I will be expected to go along the beach and creep into his house by the back way whenever he wants me, she thought with contemptuous irony; and suddenly she felt horribly, physically sick. She folded her arms around herself and leaned against the wall. She didn't want this; she didn't!

For a long time she stood there as her mind warred with her instincts. This—relationship—would be against everything she believed in, and her body cringed at the thought of his hands touching her. Couldn't she just leave the island and tell her mother that she had failed? Surely Mrs Lambert wouldn't expect this of her? But she knew with utmost certainty that her mother would not only expect it of her—she would demand it!

When she joined Ellen in the sitting-room later, dressed in a cool, short-sleeved blouse and denim skirt, she had herself under iron control, not a trace of her inner misery visible on her carefully made up face.

'There you are now,' Ellen said comfortably. 'I expect you're hungry. I heard you moving about, so I made you an omelette and salad. Come and sit you down while it's hot.'

While Felicity ate listlessly Ellen chattered on about the damage caused by the hurricane, which fortunately was slight.

'We were all far more worried about you setting out in a small boat when there was a hurricane due. What a pity you didn't wait for the answer to your radio message. Mac gave Joey and Daniel a real telling off. Daniel should have checked the forecast before you set out. Still, all's well that ends well, as the saying goes, and you are quite a heroine, my dear, performing an appendectomy in a cave, of all places!'

Felicity was content to just sit there and listen; anything to take her mind from her dilemma, but she wasn't to be left in peace.

'Bruce phoned earlier. He seemed very anxious to speak to you so I said he could call round at about eight o'clock,' Ellen told her, unaware that it was her words that had made Felicity drop her fork with a clatter. 'Have you finished? No, don't bother, I'll clear the dishes. Why don't you go and sit in the garden? You doctors always have lots of reading matter to catch up on, I ken.'

Picking up some *Therapeutics Bulletins*, Felicity wandered down to the garden seat overlooking the sea. She glanced at the magazines in a desultory way but didn't really see them. She tried not to think of anything at all, but without much success.

At five minutes to eight she saw him. He was striding along the beach to the bungalow. The fact that he was coming by the back entrance seemed morbidly significant.

He was coming nearer and had seen her now. As she watched him walk towards her it seemed to Felicity that she had been waiting many years without knowing what she was waiting for, knowing only she would recognise the moment when it came. But the thought faded with his approach; this was not it, this was not the time for which she waited.

He said lightly, 'Hello, Felicity.'

She tried to meet his eyes but couldn't, and found herself trembling again despite all her efforts to control herself.

'Let's go back to my place, shall we?'

Obediently, like a puppet, she turned and walked silently along the beach beside him. But when they got to his house he didn't attempt to take her inside, just led her to where his car was parked. He looked down at her with a strange gleam in his hard grey eyes. 'Would you like to go for a drive?'

Felicity nodded, not trusting herself to speak. He drove up into the hills, but she didn't really observe where they were going. She saw the native workers polishing the cocoa beans by dancing on them with their bare feet much as the Spanish traditionally trod grapes—'dancing cocoa', the West Indians called it. She looked at cascades of yellow cassia and golden logwood blossoms, and yet she saw nothing. She was aware only of the alien presence of the man beside her, so strong, so determined to take what he wanted.

He stopped at last and led her along a path among some trees. They came to a clearing and then she knew where she was.

'But this—this is the site for your house?' she said in bewilderment, turning to look directly at him for the first time.

A strange look passed over his face, half mocking, half tender, as he reached out to put his hands on her waist, holding her away from him so that he could see her face. 'Where else do you think I should take the girl I want to be my wife?'

'Y-your wife?' She stared at him, unable to think, to feel.

'What else did you think I intended, my sweet innocent?'

Irrationally she seized on the last word. 'I'm not innocent. I'm a doctor, and I'm twenty-five!'

'Innocence has little to do with occupation or age. It's a state of heart and mind, a quality to be guarded and cherished until you're ready to experience a deeper, lasting relationship.' He put a finger under her chin and forced her to look into his eyes. 'And you've never had such a relationship with any man, have you, Felicity?'

'N-no.' The word was wrung from her like a confession.

'I was wrong; you weren't running away from someone in England?'

'No.'

He sighed. 'I love you, Felicity. I've loved you from the moment I saw you dancing with Mac at the Residency.'

'But—but you can't ...' She couldn't bring herself to say 'love', that was too definite a word. 'You can't want to marry me. Every time we meet we argue and rub each other up the wrong way.' Agitatedly she pulled herself away from him. 'Why, at Gillian's party you were horrid to me!'

'Felicity, don't you recognise it yet? Don't you know why you tremble every time I touch you? Can't you see that this antagonism you feel is just a basic instinct to keep your independence; not to let yourself admit your real feelings?'

He pulled her roughly into his arms, his voice husky. 'Don't fight me any more, darling. I've been patiently waiting for you to know your own heart long enough. If you still don't know then that kiss during the hurricane must have told you. You knew that I'd come for you tonight, didn't you? Didn't you, Felicity?' he insisted.

'Yes.' The word was no more than a whisper. So he had thought her reaction to him had been unrecognised love, when all the time it had been hate, deep loathing hatred! She broke free of his arms. 'But you were going to marry Diane. Everyone said so.'

Slowly he answered, 'Perhaps I might have done, eventually. She's a good friend and I like her. But I saw you looking like a golden-haired Ariel and knew then that there would never be anyone else in the world for me.'

'But your career? Lady Steventon . . .'

'Cecily will just have to get used to the idea. She's really very kind-hearted, you know, and I believe she's quite fond of me. Oh, we'll probably be in her bad books for a time, but she'll come round. Especially when she sees how happy you've made me. And you are going to make me happy, aren't you, Felicity?' He tried to reach for her again, but she eluded him.

'I won't give up my work, not for anything,' she said defiantly.

'And I'll never ask you to. I was afraid that it was your love for your work that was subconsciously making you fight your feelings for me. Every time it was mentioned you were on the defensive. But I want you to have your career, just as I have mine.' For a third time he took her in his arms and this time he wasn't to be gainsaid. He looked down at her teasingly and—she realised with a queer jerk of her heart—lovingly. 'Now, Dr Felicity Lambert, is there any other possible reason you can think of why you shouldn't marry me?'

Felicity stared back at him, her face pale in the half light. There was one very good reason she could think of, but one doesn't tell one's opponent that he has just placed himself totally within your power. 'N-no,' she said slowly.

'Then will you marry me, Felicity?' his voice urgent now.

So she was to be his wife, not his mistress. Well, it made little difference. It would just make his destruction more complete, more devastating.

'Yes,' she said firmly, 'I will marry you.'

CHAPTER SIX

THE clinic at Lordstown, a small township on the eastern coast of Trenaka, was alive with the noise of dozens of children and their chattering mothers. Felicity was paying her monthly visit to give injections and generally check up on the health of the pre-school children and to answer any of the problems the mothers had. Many of the babies were crying lustily, the older ones running loose round the large room while their mothers waited their turn to see her. Often aunts and grandmothers came along as well as it was generally treated as a social event.

Felicity prescribed some ointment for a rather painful nappy rash and watched the mother amble away clutching her fat baby under her arm.

'Next one, please, nurse,' she said to the young SRN assisting her, and looked rather wearily at the still crowded room. 'Don't they ever go home?'

The coloured girl grinned at her. 'They won't go till you've seen the last one, doctor.' She brought up the next woman, a very dark-skinned West Indian who was much thinner than most of the other women; she didn't laugh or smile, either, but seemed sullen and withdrawn. A thin, large-eyed child of seven or eight clung to her skirt, his thumb stuck in his mouth. The child's eyes were watering and it appeared to have a cold. With infinite gentleness, Felicity coaxed the boy to come to her and laying him on the couch examined his chest, finding him hot and feverish.

'How long has he had this cold?' she asked the mother. The woman seemed reluctant to answer and the nurse spoke sharply to her in Creole. The woman became angry and started to shout at the nurse and Felicity in her own tongue, waving her arms about and trying to snatch the boy from the couch. The other mothers had fallen silent, but the child began to wail loudly.

'What is it? What's she saying?' Felicity asked, wishing that she could speak Creole.

The young nurse, who had trained in England, sniffed contemptuously. 'She came to Trenaka from the outer islands only a few days ago. She's a silly woman, very superstitious. She says a man with a bad-eye looked at the boy and made him ill.'

'A bad-eye?' Felicity echoed in bewilderment, and then enlightenment dawned. 'Oh, you mean evil-eye. Well, tell her she's wrong. The child seems to have influenza.'

Carefully the nurse translated Felicity's instructions for the child's care while Felicity wrote out a prescription for some antibiotics for the woman to take to a chemist. The native woman took the piece of paper gingerly and hurriedly thrust it into her pocket.

She probably thinks it's a magic formula against the 'evil-eye', Felicity thought resignedly, and made a mental note to get Mac to follow up the case. She wouldn't ask Geoff; her engagement to Bruce had put her really in the dog-house as far as Geoff was concerned.

His comments when she had told him had been scathing to say the least, and although the things he had said had hurt her, she had just had to stand there and take them.

'So you were the one who was going to be different? More interested in your career than marriage. And to think you even got me believing you!' His face was full of scorn. 'Well, I wish you joy of your marriage, Felicity. Bruce is certainly quite a catch. I just hope the poor devil knows what he's letting himself in for!' And he had slammed out of the office. Felicity had smiled mirthlessly to herself. No, she thought, Bruce doesn't know what he's letting himself in for, not yet. But soon the whole of Trenaka would know.

There had been varied reactions to the engagement announcement that Bruce had insisted on publishing in the local paper. Ellen and Mac she had told previously, of course, and they had been happy and delighted for her, although once or twice she had caught Mac giving her, a speculative look. Ellen, however, was in her element with another wedding to arrange and would have really extended herself if Felicity hadn't told her firmly that it was to be a quiet ceremony.

Gillian had gleefully phoned to congratulate her, sure in her own mind that Felicity had cunningly contrived to snatch Bruce from under Diane's nose. There had been a stiff formal note of good wishes from the Governor and Lady Steventon, and a less formal but very short note from David.

At last the clinic was over and she was able to wash her hands and tidy herself before driving back to the bungalow for dinner. Putting her powder compact back in her bag she noticed the jeweller's box with her engagement ring in it. Making the excuse that it was inconvenient to wear when she was working, she kept the ring, a large oval sapphire surrounded by diamonds, in her handbag most of the time, but she couldn't help feeling guilty whenever she had to put it on. Bruce had placed it on her finger on the very night that he had proposed to her. 'It's a family bauble,' he had said lightly. 'Given to the fiancée of the eldest son on their betrothal. I wrote to my mother and asked her to send it to me on the night that I met you.'

So he had been that sure of her, she thought bitterly. But that had been five weeks ago, and now, in just two more days, they were to be married.

Slowly she drove the Mini back along the road to Trenaka town. There were lots of men on bicycles going home from their work and she steered carefully round them. Almost half way there she pulled off the road down a side lane and switched off the engine. She needed a little time to herself, a little time to don the mask of a happy bride-to-be for Ellen's benefit. She smiled to herself. Ellen had been so disappointed when told that the ceremony was not to be held in the old stone, English-style church on the island, but in the small Register Office in the town. Almost as disappointed as Bruce had been, she thought grimly. He had taken it for granted that they would be married in the church, but Felicity had refused point blank. He had tried to persuade and cajole her, but she had been adamant. Whatever else she had to do she knew that she couldn't stand in front of an altar and make sacred vows that she had no intention of keeping.

At last Bruce had given in, but he had put up a good fight, using first Ellen and then the Reverend Gordon Wood, the island's pastor, to try to make her change her mind. Then she had become angry and told him not to bother to arrange any wedding at all and had thrust the ring back at him.

His lips had tightened and he looked so furious that she thought he was going to shake her, but he merely said harshly, 'Don't be a fool.' He took the ring from her palm where she held it out to him and put it back on her finger, then, still holding her hand, he raised it to his lips and kissed each of her fingers in turn. Before he had reached the third one she could feel her hand shaking. 'Don't ever do that again.' His voice was no longer angry and there was a wry smile on his lips. 'All right, Felicity, you win. If that's the way you want it, we'll be married in a civil ceremony. You'd better tell Ellen before she invites the whole of Trenaka. There will never be room for them all in that little room at the Register Office.'

But as it worked out they weren't to be married in the Register Office after all, for the Governor had stepped in and insisted that the Residency be used for the ceremony, as it, too, was licensed for marriages. It seemed then only natural that Lady Steventon should come forward with an offer of the Residency lawn for the reception, and Felicity guessed that Bruce must have exerted all his charm, for she was sure that he was behind the offer; the musty little Register Office hadn't pleased him at all. But in this she did Lady Steventon an injustice, for both Sir Miles and his wife held Bruce in great affection, and although they didn't approve of his marriage, they were willing to make the best of it for his sake.

Beyond writing a polite note of thanks to them both, Felicity had left everything in Ellen's capable hands, dissociating herself from the arrangements as far as she was able and, like Mac, fleeing from the house to the hospital as it began to fill with acceptance cards, presents, and long lists that Ellen was continuously writing out. Maybe that was why Mac gave Felicity those strange looks.

One of the hardest parts had been trying to decide whether or not to write and tell her mother the news. She had dithered over the problem and then decided to wait until everything was over. Bruce had given her a nasty jolt one day when he asked her if she would like her aunt to come out to Trenaka for the wedding.

'Oh, no,' Felicity had said, too hastily. 'That won't be necessary.'

'Wouldn't she like to see you married?'

'She wouldn't leave England,' she replied positively. 'She hates to travel and—and really, we're not all that close.'

At the time she had said it as an excuse, but now she knew that it had been true. Absence from her mother had made her realise the shallowness of their relationship, the lack of any real depth of feeling on her mother's part.

'What about your mother?' she had forced herself to ask. 'Will she be coming?'

'Unfortunately, no. My sister is expecting her third child very soon and naturally wants my mother with her.'

Felicity felt a wave of relief; she didn't remember ever meeting Mrs Gresham, but there was always the possibility that his mother might have recognised her.

'She's very disappointed, of course, as I am,' Bruce continued. 'But I certainly don't intend to wait until she's free to come to Trenaka to claim my bride. I don't think I could wait that long.'

Felicity had flushed and looked away. For a few moments he studied her averted face and then kissed his fingers and placed them under her chin in the gesture she was rapidly becoming used to. She supposed that he had been very patient with her, sensing (but for the wrong reasons) that she was a bag of nerves, constantly poised on the edge of running away from this marriage he had almost coerced her into accepting. Although he had kissed her often, they had been light gentle kisses. He had not been ruthlessly demanding as on the night of the hurricane.

It seemed so long ago that night, almost like a film you had seen, the details blurred and only the basic facts lingering in the memory to be recalled once or twice and then lost until something made you remember them again sharply and clearly. Felicity sighed, then glancing at her watch realised she would have to hurry or she would be late for dinner. Mac was going to the Club in Trenaka town that night for Bruce's stag party celebration, while Ellen was going to the Residency to make some final arrangements for the wedding with Lady Steventon.

Over dinner she told Mac about the little native boy who had been brought to the clinic in Lordstown.

'You'll come across that quite often, but mostly on the smaller, more remote islands. They all believe in a laddie called the Spider, who was supposed to have travelled across the Atlantic with captive slaves from Ashantiland. Then there are spirits—Diablesses—who are supposed to slay men by taking them into the heart of the forest and putting a spell on them; and Legawas who shed their skins and suck the blood of anybody they can catch.' Mac made a fearsome, leering face so that Felicity had to laugh at him, but Ellen said crossly,

'Now then, that's enough of your blather. You'll frighten

Felicity to death and she'll have nightmares instead of getting a good night's sleep. Why, the lass looks tired out already, and I won't have her with bags under her eyes for the wedding.'

Mac winked at Felicity, but added seriously, 'Don't worry about the bairn. Whenever a child gets a fever they blame it on the bad-eye.'

'Well, it looked remarkably like nothing more than 'flu to me,' Felicity said with a laugh.

''Flu?' There was a slight frown between Mac's brows, but Felicity didn't notice it, for Ellen had called her attention to one of her lists.

'Now the photographs, dear. Do you want them taken inside the Residency or outside in the grounds?'

'Well, inside, I suppose. Or perhaps outside would be better? Oh, I don't know, Ellen. I'll leave it to you. I'm sure you know what's best. I must write up these progress reports.' And picking up her medical bag she escaped to her room.

Presently she heard the car drive away as Ellen dropped Mac off before driving on to the Residency. She went back into the living-room and tried to interest herself in a magazine, but put it down again in a few minutes and wandered restlessly about the room. Selecting a record, she put it on the stereo, but it soon played a love theme, so she snapped it off angrily and put the 1812 Overture on instead, very loudly, so that she didn't have to listen to herself think, then lay back in the armchair and let the rousing music roll over her.

The bells were teeming out their victory peals and the guns firing in happy accord so that she didn't hear a car drive up and a knock on the door, and she jumped in fright when she felt a light touch on her arm. Opening her eyes, she saw Diane Cunningham looking down at her uncertainly.

'I'm so sorry, I didn't hear you come in. The music ...' Hurriedly she got to her feet and went to turn off the stereo. 'I'm afraid Ellen isn't here, she's gone to the Residency to see Lady Steventon. But surely you know ...' Felicity broke off, wondering why the other girl had come here.

'Yes. Yes, I did know. That's why I came tonight. I knew that both Dr and Mrs MacAllister would be out. I—I wanted to talk to you.' Diane clutched her handbag in both hands and Felicity realised that she was very nervous. Immediately her professional training came to the fore and she tried to put Diane at ease.

'Won't you sit down? I was just going to have a Planter's Punch; will you join me?'

Diane nodded and Felicity hastily poured the drinks. She knew the basic ingredients but had never made the drink before so, without realising it, she put in rather large measures of rum. She handed a glass to Diane, who thanked her politely. Going to her chair, Felicity looked at her guiltily; Diane had every reason to hate her for taking Bruce away, and she wondered uneasily if she had come to tell her so, to tell her exactly what she thought of her.

Slowly, and with obvious difficulty, Diane said, 'I expect when you first came here that you noticed that Bruce and I went to parties and things together quite a lot?'

'Yes, I suppose I did,' Felicity said with a sinking heart, fearful that Diane might hurt herself even more if she gave way to her feelings.

'I believe there were rumours at the time. Rumours about —about Bruce and myself, that is. Well, I ...'

'Look,' Felicity broke in awkwardly, 'please don't go on.'

'Oh, but I must.' Diane thrust her chin forward determinedly and Felicity sighed and sat back in her chair, ready to take whatever Diane meted out to her.

'I know that there were—certain people who hoped for a —a connection between us, and we were—we are—quite friendly. But I wanted to tell you myself that there was never really anything between us. I'm sure that Bruce has done so already, but it's been on my mind that you might

104

be worried that there'd been an attachment, that Bruce might still have some feelings for me. But I assure you that there was absolutely nothing.' She looked at Felicity earnestly, with a worried frown, afraid that she might not be believed.

It was so completely the opposite of what she had expected that for a few moments Felicity could only gaze at Diane while she tried to assimilate what had been said. Then she flushed with embarrassment and took a hasty swallow of her drink. That Diane should have been worried about *her* feelings; should have laid bare the details of their friendship so that Felicity could feel at ease! Felicity felt lower than a worm and hastily rose to pour out more drinks so that Diane couldn't see her face.

'Diane, I don't know what to say. It was a very—remarkable thing to do, to come here and say that, and it took a very remarkable person to do it. Bruce told me that you were great friends—now I can see why.'

The older girl flushed with pleasure and busied herself with her drink. It seemed to give her a little Dutch courage, because she said confidingly, 'As a matter of fact I know I would never have been really happy as the wife of a senior official, even if Bruce had ever asked me. You see, I'm basically rather shy, and although I don't mind organising parties and arranging functions, I get awfully nervous when I have to meet important people. I'm always so petrified that I'll say the wrong thing that I just sit there and don't say a word.'

'Good heavens, Diane, I had no idea. But why do you stay here if you hate it so?'

'When my mother died I had nowhere else to go.' She emptied her glass and Felicity automatically rose to refill it. 'Cecily took me under her wing, and, I suppose because she had no children of her own, she became very ambitious for me, and as Sir Miles was so fond of Bruce it seemed only natural that she should try to bring us together. I had no qualifications, no career, you see.' She sighed rather sadly and sipped her drink. 'Not like you! I do envy you, Felicity, you're so self-confident and you have your independence; you don't have to rely on the kindness of relations for a home and livelihood. Why, you don't even have to marry if you don't want to, whereas that's the only thing left open to me if I'm not to be at Cecily's beck and call for the rest of my life.'

If Felicity had ever had any doubts about what she was doing, she had them now. If she hadn't come to Trenaka thirsting for revenge, Bruce and Diane would eventually have married and Diane would at least have had a home of her own and not be Lady Steventon's charity object. And Bruce would have been kind to her, even if he hadn't been in love with her, of that Felicity was somehow sure.

As Diane relaxed she talked of her childhood in the west country. 'Do you know what I would really like to do?' she said with a wistful giggle. 'I'd love to run a market garden.'

'A market garden?' Felicity choked. 'Oh, Diane, no wonder you can't stand the Residency!'

'I know, it's completely ludicrous.'

There were no longer any barriers between them and they talked and laughed for another hour before Diane left to drive home. They had had another couple of drinks and Diane's car jerked and weaved along the road somewhat as she headed for the Residency.

Slowly Felicity washed the glasses, the temporary happy mood obliterated with Diane's going. She admired Diane for coming to see her and it sharpened her own feelings of guilt. The need for vengeance seemed to pale into insignificance when she thought of Diane having to live the rest of her life in a manner she hated. But perhaps it wasn't too late! Abruptly she threw down the tea-towel, and going into her bedroom pulled a couple of suitcases out of the wardrobe. Hastily she began to throw some clothes into them together with her more treasured bits and pieces. Then she changed into a travelling suit.

There was a knock at the door and Ellen poked her head

106

round. 'Are you in bed, dear?' She broke off in consternation as she saw the packed suitcases. 'Felicity, what on earth are you doing?'

'I'm leaving! I'm sorry, Ellen, but I'm not going through with it.' She tried to say it emphatically, but somehow her voice seemed slurred.

Ellen looked at her with growing comprehension. 'Diane got back to the Residency just before I left. She said she'd been to see you. I think, maybe, you had a wee dram or two?'

'We had a couple of Planter's Punches. What's that got to do with it?' Felicity asked, puzzled. 'Ellen, will you be a dear and drive me to the airport? I should have time to catch the night plane to Jamaica, if I hurry.'

'I'm afraid I don't feel like turning out again tonight. You had best wait till the morning and give yourself time to think it over.'

'I don't want to think it over,' Felicity said fiercely. 'Oh, Ellen, I'm truly sorry that I've upset all your plans, but don't you see? It was all a terrible mistake and I just can't go through with it!' Ellen thought she meant the marriage, of course, but Felicity really meant the events she had planned for after the wedding ceremony.

'Very well,' said Ellen, coming to a decision. 'If that's the way you feel, then I'll telephone for transport for you.'

She went away while Felicity finished packing and collected her medical bag. Should she write a note for Bruce? What could she put beyond the bald facts: 'I don't want to marry you. I'm leaving.' She certainly had no intention of telling him the truth and she only hoped that he and Diane would get together again. She heard a car draw up outside and carried her cases into the sitting-room. There was no sign of Ellen. Perhaps she has gone on to the veranda, Felicity thought, hating to have to say goodbye to the woman who had been so truly kind to her, and hating herself for the hasty way she was saying those goodbyes.

Ellen wasn't on the veranda and Felicity called out to

the driver, a tall shadow standing by his car in the darkness, 'Put my cases in, will you? I won't be a moment.'

She went to walk past him to look for Ellen in the garden, but as she passed he moved with deceptive swiftness and caught her wrist, pulling her round to face him.

'Bruce!' Felicity went cold inside. 'Why—why are you here?'

'Ellen sent for me. She seemed to think I was needed.' He looked down at her frightened face and then tucked her arm through his so that she had to follow him. 'Let's go down to the beach, shall we?'

'Bruce, please, you don't understand.'

'Don't I? I assure you I do.' They had reached the beach, but she was deaf to the sound of the surf and the gentle sigh of the breeze in the palm trees. He looked very immaculate in his black evening suit, but there was an odd glint in his eyes that scared her. 'So you and Diane had a talk, did you? A heart-to-heart which ended with Diane driving straight across the sacred turf of the Residency lawn and ending up almost in the fountain, and you packing your bags and heading for the first flight for England! I don't know what you put in those drinks, Felicity, but my stag night celebrations have certainly paled in comparison.'

Felicity stared at him. He was laughing at her! How dare he? Angrily she tried to wrench herself away from him, but he wouldn't let her go and laughed openly. Raising her free hand, she beat fiercely at his chest, but he caught and held her easily, forcing her arms behind her back and imprisoning both her wrists in his one hand.

He looked down at her, still laughing. 'Little spitfire! I shall enjoy taming you.' Then with a smile on his lips, he said more gently, 'Oh, my sweet, intoxicated darling! Do you really think I would have let you go? You made a promise, remember?' He bent his head and kissed the side of her neck and she felt herself quiver as he touched her. 'Don't you know that wherever you had run to I would have gone after you and brought you back?'

'You would have followed me?' She stared at him, the sense of inevitability beginning to envelop her once again.

'Of course.'

She made one last desperate try. 'Bruce, you've got to let me go.'

'Never! Nothing and no one, not even you, my darling, is going to stop me making you my wife.' He pulled her to him and she felt his lean powerfulness against her. Slowly he kissed the curve of her chin, the hollows of her cheeks, her eyelids, taking all the time in the world about it, letting her know that she was subject to his will, that in less than forty-eight hours she would belong to him completely.

But even as her body trembled with awareness as he caressed her, she forced her brain to remember, over and over again, that in just a few days she would be rid of Bruce and Trenaka for ever!

Bruce's boat, the *Salamander*, was waiting for them when they finally reached the quayside and someone had covered the mast, the rigging, rails, every available surface with ribbons and flowers.

'Just look at that! What a perfect way to go on a honeymoon—in a boat covered with flowers!' Ellen cried. 'I must get Mac to take a photograph.' She bustled away to find Mac among the crowd of well-wishers who had followed them in a procession of cars from the reception at the Residency to see them off on their honeymoon.

Now the guests were laughing as they pelted the bridal couple with rice and confetti. Grinning fishermen roared with laughter and children ran among their legs picking up the fallen scraps of paper to throw them at one another. Mac made them pose for a last photograph and then Felicity was saying goodbye to everyone; Diane, David, the Marshs, the Sinclairs, and hugging Mac and Ellen, thanking them for all they had done, before Bruce firmly took her arm and almost lifted her off the quayside on to the boat. David, who had been their best man, cast off the mooring rope, Bruce started the engine and the *Salamander* began to nose out of the harbour as the other boats hooted and blew their whistles for them. Felicity stood clinging to the rail, waving until they were out of the harbour into the open sea.

Everyone had been so wonderfully kind. Sir Miles and Lady Steventon had given them a splendid wedding present and their good wishes had been sincere. Even Geoff had unbent sufficiently to insist on kissing the bride and had come to see them off with Edwina Draycott, whom Felicity had invited. Ellen and Mac—of course, it went without saying. She felt almost overwhelmed as she remembered the way they had encouraged and helped her to get through the day, from Mac letting her hold tightly to his hand while giving her away, to Ellen helping her to change from her wedding dress into the cream linen suit and sleeveless blouse she now wore. They had waved her away so gaily, expecting them to be gone for at least three weeks. It would be a terrible shock for them when Felicity turned up the next day!

She bit her lip; better not to think about that now. She had planned it all down to the last detail and knew exactly what she had to do. In just a few hours it would all be over. But how she hated the thought of having to deceive the friends who had been so kind to her.

Slowly she turned and went to join Bruce in the cockpit; she must play her part in this masquerade for a little while longer yet. He, too, had changed and wore a navy blazer and white trousers. He held out his free hand to her and she barely hesitated before going to stand at his side.

'What course are we taking?' She made her voice casual, but the question was all-important. Soon she would be making the return journey alone and she must be sure of finding her way.

'We sail due west for twenty-five miles and then alter

course to N.N.W. for about four miles till we come to Jabalya Key.'

This was a tiny coral island that had been lent to Bruce by a friend, Tony Maidment, for their honeymoon. It had a small but luxurious bungalow built on it—and that alone. There were no other buildings and no other people. 'What a perfect place for a honeymoon,' Ellen had said when told of it. 'So very romantic to be alone together on an island.' Felicity had supposed that it would be romantic if that was what they had been going there for, but as it was it would suit her purpose very well.

'Would you like to take the wheel for a while?'

Gingerly Felicity did so. She had only piloted Bruce's boat once before for a very short time and she had taken care that he shouldn't find out that she had learned to handle the hospital motor boat, but it wouldn't do any harm to get the feel of the *Salamander* before she took it out alone.

'What are all the dials and gauges for?'

Patiently he explained each one, putting a casual arm across her shoulders and watching her progress. 'You know, Mrs Gresham, I think we'll make a sailor of you yet.' His fingers tightened on her shoulder and he rested his cheek against the clean-smelling softness of her hair.

Abruptly Felicity took her hands off the wheel and he caught it hastily before it could spin round. 'I'm so hot. I think I'll go into the cabin and take off my jacket.'

'Good idea. Take mine with you, will you?' He slipped an arm out of the blazer and Felicity held it as he took it off. Underneath he was wearing a loose-knit shirt and she could see the hard muscles rippling beneath it. Quickly she turned away and went into the cabin with its bunks on either side. Bruce was so physically strong that he could overpower her easily. If he found out; if anything went wrong ...? But nothing could go wrong. She was sure that she had thought of every eventuality. Fiercely she gripped her fists and longed for it all to be over.

111

She stayed in the cabin as long as she dared, but eventually went back into the cockpit. He made no comment on her tardiness, merely gave her a quick glance and began to talk of the wedding reception. Here she was safe and could converse freely with him. Indeed, a couple of times he made her laugh as he recalled some amusing incidents. During their conversation he had changed course and Felicity saw a smudge of land appear on the horizon. She broke off an animated description of Ellen's panic when she thought she had lost Felicity's bouquet, only to find that Mac had put it in the fridge to keep fresh, and fell silent, her hand gripping the rail tightly. Leaning forward, Bruce loosened her fingers and gently played with them, his hand warm and strong.

'We'll soon be there,' he said easily, and Felicity looked at him, her face pale and her eyes unnaturally bright. He gave her an encouraging grin and she managed a small, weak smile in return.

It *was* a perfect place. A small atoll with palm trees, a curving beach of white coral sand around a peaceful lagoon, and a beautifully appointed bungalow that even had electricity powered by its own generator.

'Who looks after it?' Felicity asked. 'Surely your friend doesn't leave it empty when he's away?'

'No, there's a very efficient couple who look after the place for him, but he gave them a holiday after they got the bungalow ready and stocked up for us.' Bruce had brought their cases ashore and was now bringing in their diving equipment from the boat.

'What would you like to do first; explore, eat or unpack?'

'I don't feel hungry yet. I think I'd like to unpack first and then explore.'

'Fine.' He carried the cases into the bedroom and Felicity followed him. The room was dominated by a huge double bed, at least six feet wide, and Felicity felt herself blushing as Bruce grinned. 'Tony certainly gets his priorities right, doesn't he?'

After they had unpacked they walked round the island, which was only about two miles from end to end, roughly in the shape of a crescent moon.

'Do you see those rocks down there?' Bruce pointed. 'We'll be able to go fishing there, it looks a good spot.'

'But I don't know how to fish,' she objected.

'Then I'll teach you.' He raised her hand to his lips, turning it so that he pressed a kiss deep into her palm. 'Hungry yet?'

'Yes, I am rather. I hope Tony's servants have kept a well-stocked larder.'

They had indeed. In addition to the fridge, there was a freezer full of food and cupboards of tinned goods of every variety.

'You can cook, I suppose?' Bruce asked her teasingly.

'Of course not,' she managed somehow to play along with his light mood.

'In that case we shall probably starve, because I can't either.'

'You should have thought of that before you chose a desert island. Go away, while I try to concoct something.'

He grinned and kissed her bare shoulder—oh, so casually —before he went away to secure the boat.

The concoction was steak with mushrooms, tomatoes and a tossed green salad, with guavas to follow. Bruce ate appreciatively, but Felicity hardly touched her food, merely pushing it around her plate. He had opened a bottle of Burgundy and they each had a couple of glasses. With apparent equanimity, Bruce talked calmly of the amusements they would find on the island, but a sharp throb began to tap at the side of Felicity's throat, a sure sign that her nerves were at screaming point.

As soon as they had finished she rose abruptly and said, 'I'll make some coffee. Shall we have it in the sitting-room?' Putting the dirty dishes on a tray, she carried it out to the kitchen. The time would soon be here; she must try and keep calm, but her hands were shaking as she prepared the coffee and carried the tray back into the sitting-room where Bruce sprawled nonchalantly on the sofa. Felicity poured him a cup but took her own over to the window to watch the sunset. It never ceased to amaze her that the sun could go down so quickly here. One moment it was bright day and within a short space it was dark night; there was hardly any twilight as in England. She gave a little sigh; the time had come.

Bruce came to stand beside her and she jumped as he put his arm round her waist. 'I thought we might drink a toast.'

He had brought a bottle of champagne from the fridge and she jumped again as the cork popped. He filled two glasses and handed one to her. 'To us, my beautiful girl. To our future together.' He drank the toast, watching her while he did so. Felicity lifted the glass to her lips, but she only pretended to drink.

'Felicity . . .' he began, but she quickly interrupted him.

'I've just remembered; I left something on the boat. Have you locked it up? Can I have the keys so that I can fetch it?'

'Won't it do in the morning?'

'No, I'd rather get it now,' she said firmly.

'Then I'll fetch it for you. Where is it?'

'Please, Bruce, I'd rather go myself. It's a—a sort of surprise.'

He looked at her in some amusement and then took the boat keys from his pocket and put them in her hand. She closed her fingers round them tightly. He put his hands low on her hips and drew her close, his lips seeking hers possessively, as if he owned her. She let him do what he wanted. It was the last time she would ever have to yield to his disgusting caresses!

'Hurry back, wife,' he said thickly.

He let her go at last and she turned and hurried out of the room, pausing only to wipe her mouth with the back of her hand. Once outside the bungalow she ran breathlessly

114

through the darkness along the path to the jetty. Thanks to her exploration this afternoon she was confident of finding her way quite easily.

It had been so easy! He had given her the keys with hardly any argument. Now all she had to do was to sail the boat away from the island and out of his life for ever! It was difficult running on the soft sand, so she stopped for a moment to pull off her shoes. Yes, that was better. The stars shone brilliantly in a clear sky, she could have steered by them if she hadn't had a compass.

Her stockinged feet made no noise as she ran along the wooden jetty and cast off the mooring ropes before jumping lightly down on to the deck of the boat. In a few hours she would be back in Trenaka—alone! She could imagine the astonished expressions of the people who first saw her, the wild rumours and gossiping scandal that would spread like wildfire throughout the island. At first, when she had been planning what she would do, she had thought of several different stories she could tell to explain her hasty return from her honeymoon, but then it had gradually dawned on her that she didn't have to say anything at all. If she just pretended to be in deep shock and refused to say a word, then everyone would fill in the gaps from their own fertile imaginations, especially when she absolutely refused even to see Bruce again!

With deep satisfaction she savoured the thought of the humiliation he would feel when they had to send a boat out to pick him up. How his denials that there was anything wrong would only increase the surmise and conjecture about him. It would most certainly go down against him on his record; how could they possibly promote a man who had terrified his bride into running away from him on their wedding night! And she intended to act very, very terrified!

Going into the cockpit, she put the key into the ignition and pressed the starter, her heart beating wildly with excitement. The engine didn't fire. She pressed the starter again, but still the wretched thing hadn't caught. Perhaps it needed more fuel. Felicity pulled out the choke and tried again. Still nothing happened. Oh, no! Oh, God, please don't let it break down now, not now, she prayed. Everything depended on her getting away tonight!

Biting her lip, Felicity tried to keep calm and think clearly; the engine hadn't turned at all, it seemed to be completely dead. Could it be the batteries? Hastily she pulled off the cover over the engine housing, but it was too dark to see properly and the light in the cockpit wouldn't come on when she pressed the switch. Surely the whole electrical system hadn't fused? Bruce kept a torch on a hook, so she quickly took it down and shone it on the batteries. They looked all right, but the connections might have come loose. She took a spanner from the tool-box and kneeling on the deck with her head in the hole, did them up as tight as she could.

Beads of perspiration stood out on her forehead and she wiped them away with her hand, then jumped up hopefully to try the ignition again. Hardly daring to breathe, she pressed the starter. Nothing! It was as dead as before. Oh, no! She threw the torch down and gripped the wheel in despair. The boat lurched as someone jumped aboard and Felicity turned, to cry out in terror as Bruce appeared in the doorway.

'It's all right, it's only me.' There was laughter in his voice as he spoke, but his expression changed to one of amazement as he saw the open hatch cover. 'What on earth ...?' Then he noticed the keys still swinging in the ignition. 'What the hell are you trying to do?' he questioned, and came purposefully towards her.

Felicity snatched at the spanner she had been using and cowered back into the corner. 'No, don't touch me!'

He stopped short, appalled. 'Felicity, what is it? What's the matter?' He stared at her white face and frightened eyes. 'You were trying to start the boat, weren't you? That's why the mooring lines were loose. You were going to leave without a word,' he added unbelievingly, then grimly, 'All right, Felicity, let's have it. Just where did you think you were going?'

Numbly she stared at him. She'd got to have time to think, time to try and save something from the dreadful turn that events had taken.

'Answer me, Felicity! Where the hell were you going?'

'B-back to Trenaka.'

He stared at her wordlessly, then moved towards her, but she hastily brandished the spanner. 'Don't come near me!' she yelled in panic. A hysterical gurgle came to her lips and suddenly she was laughing and crying at the same time, unnatural bursts of laughter that racked her whole body. Why hadn't the boat started? Why?

'Felicity, stop it! Pull yourself together.' With one quick movement he had pulled the spanner from her hands, then he took hold of her shoulders and shook her vigorously.

Immediately she stopped laughing, but tremors of emotion still ran through her. White-faced, she looked up at him, her eyes full of hate. 'Take your hands away from me!' she said fiercely.

Slowly he did so, watching her intently. 'Why were you trying to run out on me?' His eyes blazed with suppressed anger.

Felicity licked her suddenly dry lips. She couldn't tell him the truth; not here, not when she was completely alone with him. Already there was a hard, grim look on his face and she was terrified of what he might do to her, what form his rage might take, if he found out that she had been deceiving him all along. She would have to play a part; make him think anything but the truth.

'I'm—I'm afraid I made a ghastly mistake. I should never have married you at all.'

There was a brief shattering silence as they stood there, facing one another in the small cockpit. Then, keeping a tight hold on himself, Bruce said, 'We can't discuss this

117

here. Let's go back to the bungalow and we'll talk about it over a drink.'

'No, I'm not going anywhere with you,' she panicked. 'I've told you it's all a mistake. I can't go through with it! You've got to let me go!'

'Are you crazy?' he said tensely. 'All right, I know I rushed you into this, but we're husband and wife now, and we're going to stay that way!' He tried to pull her towards him, to take her in his arms.

Knowing how she went to pieces when he touched her, Felicity struggled desperately against him. 'No, don't touch me!' The boat lurched beneath them and she fell against the chart table, hurting her side.

She gave a little cry of pain and then Bruce was half carrying her into the cabin and sitting her on the port bunk. 'Now tell me what the hell this is all about,' he said savagely, his breathing heavy.

Felicity lifted an ashen face up to him and tried to play for time to think. 'Bruce, I'm sorry. But I just can't— can't . . .'

He sat down beside her and picked up her hand, twisting the shiny gold band that he had put on her finger such a short time ago. 'Felicity, this isn't just wedding nerves. You've been as jumpy as a cat ever since we got engaged, that's why I've held back, hoping you would get over it. Perhaps it would have been better if I'd shown you what love was a little more.' He sighed. 'Darling, there has to be some reason other than nerves for you trying to run away. You should have told me before—but now you've *got* to tell me, you realise that?'

'Yes,' she whispered, seeking desperately for something that would satisfy him, make him leave her alone.

'Then why, dearest, why are you so frightened of men?'

It was his choice of words that gave her the idea, and it was so simple. 'When—when I was very young,' she faltered. 'A—a man . . .'

She heard his swift intake of breath and she didn't have

118

to say any more, he filled in the rest himself.

'A man assaulted you? Oh, my poor girl. I always thought that a man had hurt you in some way, but I thought it was recently, never that ... I'd like to ...' He stopped abruptly, a grim set to his mouth. 'How old were you?'

'Fifteen,' Felicity said quietly, and it was true in a way. She had been assaulted by a man then. By Bruce himself. Not physically, as he thought, of course. But he had taken the brother she loved and ruined her previously happy childhood, tearing her and her mother away from their home and shattering their peace. The thought filled her with iron resolve. If she could keep him at a distance and make him feel sorry for her, there might still be a chance to get away on the boat and fulfil her plan after all.

He swore under his breath, then put up his hand to stroke her hair gently. 'Why didn't you tell me?'

Felicity looked down at her hands clasped tightly in her lap. 'I thought I could go through with it, but when it came to it, I—I knew that I couldn't.'

'Darling, there's nothing to be afraid of. I love you. I'm not going to hurt you.' His mouth touched her hair.

'No, Bruce, I can't!' Her voice rose hysterically again. 'I want to go back to Trenaka. I can't stay here with you.'

His hand closed tightly on her hers for a moment. 'You're too tense and on edge to think straight,' he said roughly. 'We're going back to the bungalow and you're going to get a good night's sleep. We'll talk about this again in the morning when you're feeling better.'

He helped her to her feet and she looked up into his face thrown into sharp relief by the moonlight. 'You—you won't ...?'

His voice was grim. 'Not until you're ready. Not until you want it as much as I do.'

So she had won her breathing space, she thought with relief as they climbed on to the jetty. Won herself some time to work out an alternative plan. At the end of the jetty she turned to look back at the boat. 'Why wouldn't it start?' she asked.

Bruce looked at her for a moment. 'It has an anti-theft lock which needs a special key. It cuts out the entire electrical system.'

So that was it; a simple lock that she hadn't known about had ruined all her careful planning, she thought bitterly. Now she was virtually his prisoner. 'And where is the key?'

His voice was harsh. 'In my pocket, and that's where it's going to stay until we both leave here together.' He took a firm hold of her arm and led her back towards the house.

CHAPTER SEVEN

AFTER a restless night, Felicity woke the next morning in the big bed and wondered fleetingly where she was, then memory came flooding back. On their return from the boat Bruce had made them both hot milk drinks, said, 'Go to bed, little one. Don't worry, we'll work something out.' Then he had kissed her gently and gone to sleep in the spare bedroom. And Felicity had gone into the main bedroom with a strangely empty feeling inside.

She had slept late and threw open the shutters to let in the bright sunshine. The swimming pool looked cool and inviting, so she quickly changed into a swimsuit and plunged deep into its depths, trying not to think of what the coming day might bring. The bottom of the kidney-shaped pool was lined with mirrors and Felicity could see herself as she swam along, her slender brown body in the lime-green suit and her golden hair floating out around her head like a cloud. Bruce, too, had been swimming, but now he sat on a lounger at the side and watched her until she was too tired to swim any more and had to come out. Her beach towel lay on another lounger side by side with his. Momentarily she thought of going back to the bungalow to dry herself in the bathroom. Then she squared her shoulders and walked towards him; this moment had to be faced. Picking up the towel, she sat on the lounger and wrapped the towel turban fashion round her hair.

'Cigarette?'

'Please.' Her hand shook only slightly as she took one from the gold case he held out to her, but his didn't waver as he lit it for her. His eyes rested for a moment on her white face and the dark shadows round her eyes, his mouth set in a tight line, but he made no comment. Lying back on the lounger and drawing on the cigarette, Felicity thought that despite herself, as a doctor she had to admire his fantastic will-power; what he was going through she could only guess at.

'What do you think of the mirrored floor? A nice conceit, don't you think?'

'Yes, most unusual.'

'Tony has a flair for that sort of thing. One of his interests is designing and he likes to add novel touches here and there. I thought of asking him for some ideas for our house, when we start to build it.'

With thumping heart Felicity waited for him to go on, but after finishing his cigarette he stood up and said, 'Let's eat, shall we? I expect you're hungry. I know I am.'

'No, I'll just stay here. You go ahead.'

'Starving yourself isn't going to improve the situation, Felicity. Or did you intend that we eat in relays?' he said sardonically.

Reluctantly she got to her feet and he waited for her to walk along beside him, talking easily of other innovations that Tony had introduced. But Felicity didn't join in the conversation. She had to hold aloof from him; she knew that if she relented one iota towards him he would take full advantage of her weakness.

'I thought we might eat on the terrace.' His voice made her jump and she knew that he had been watching her closely. 'Come and help me carry the things from the kitchen.'

He had already prepared breakfast and there was coffee percolating on the cooker. They carried the things through to the terrace and Felicity found that she was, in fact, very hungry. Over the last few days, and yesterday especially, the nervous tension had built up so much that she had eaten very little. She finished the last crumb of her second crusty roll and sat back in her chair, feeling almost relaxed as the sun dried her still damp hair.

'Feeling better?' The question was casually asked, but Felicity knew that he was not to be put off any longer. Slowly she put her cup and saucer back on the table; the masquerade must begin again. 'Darling, if one of your patients came to you and told you that she was afraid to face up to married life because of something that happened to her ten years before, how would you advise her?' he asked unexpectedly.

Felicity took a quick look at his intent face and then hastily looked away again. It was a clever question, she realised; by making her look at herself from a professional viewpoint he hoped that she would be able to overcome her pretended abhorrence of men. But he wasn't going to gain anything that way.

'I don't know,' she said flatly.

'But I think you do.' He took hold of her hand before she could draw it away and held it firmly, looking at her steadily. 'What would you tell her, Felicity?'

'I tell you I don't know!' Then, as he continued to watch her, 'I—I might tell her that all men aren't the same, I suppose,' she faltered.

'Go on, what else?'

'How can I say? It would depend on the circumstances.' Agitatedly she tried to stand up, but he wouldn't let go of her hand and she had to sit down again. She mustn't let him involve her in any theological argument because she knew she would lose. He would make her accept his reasoning, and once accepted ... She had to hold out against him, she had to!

'Wouldn't you also tell her that she couldn't let something—no matter how terrible at the time—stand in the way of her present happiness?'

Felicity's hand moved restlessly within his like an imprisoned butterfly. 'Perhaps. I don't know. Stop acting like

123

a psychiatrist.' She turned pleading eyes towards him. 'Please, Bruce, don't go on.'

'It's got to be faced,' he insisted. 'You've got to learn to trust me,' he said urgently.

She looked away and he let go of her hand at last. She hastily took it away and began to pleat the edge of the tablecloth nervously.

'Look at me, Felicity.' His voice was commanding and she slowly raised her head, her hair still damp on her brow. 'Do you believe that I love you?'

A frightened, hunted look came into her eyes and she tried to look away, but he held hers with his own. 'Do you, Felicity?'

Briefly she nodded.

'Then surely you know that I wouldn't do anything to hurt you. You have to trust me!'

She became absorbed in the tablecloth again. 'Just what does trusting you entail?' she said, her voice cautious.

His eyes lightened a little. 'I thought that perhaps we could look upon this as just an ordinary holiday for a while, not a honeymoon,' he said carefully. 'We can still enjoy ourselves on the island as we intended to, but without any—emotional involvement—unless you want it. I realise that I hurried you into this marriage before you were really ready and that we've had very little chance to be together since our engagement, but this will give us a chance to get to know one another, to learn to trust each other.'

'If we're going to trust one another then I think you ought to give me the key to the boat to look after,' Felicity said, her heart beating so loudly that she felt he must hear it.

He studied her face for a time. 'No, you're too apt to run away from a situation you can't handle,' he said gravely. 'You must trust me with the key, too.'

She stood up abruptly. 'I'm going for a walk.'

'Would you like me to come with you?'

'No! Sharply. Then, 'I—I'm sorry. I just wanted to be by myself,' she apologised.

He nodded, and she turned and walked off towards the beach alone.

For a long time she sat on the sand near a rock pool, observing the small creatures that lived there. Her head ached abominably and she wanted to go and hide herself away like the tiny fish that burrowed down into the sand until they were completely buried. How long could she go on in this situation, she wondered, even in the circumstances that Bruce had outlined? He would try to wear her down, she knew, but there was too much tension between them for anything even approaching a natural, friendly relationship to be regained. Not that there ever had been friendliness between them. No, they had always struck too many sparks off each other for that; Bruce because he had fallen in love with her and wanted her, and Felicity because she hated him so much.

Trying to think of the best way to handle things, she decided that she would have to appear to make some effort towards meeting him half way. If she antagonised him too much he might lose his temper with her, however much he held himself in check now. And heaven knows what would happen then! She shivered, realising just how much she was at his mercy, here, alone on the island with him. If she thwarted him, or goaded him too far ... he might take matters into his own hands. He might force her to let him make love to her. Because he wanted her very much, that she knew. She had known it every time he had kissed her, touched her, caressed her.

The long feathery branches of the casuarina trees swayed in the breeze and she shivered with genuine cold now, aware that she was still only wearing her swimsuit and a thin shirt. She had been here for hours. There was the sound of music coming from the kitchen when she got back to the bungalow, but she made straight for the bedroom to get some clean clothes before taking a bath.

Opening the wardrobe to get out a dress, she saw that the clothes Bruce had hung in there only the day before had been removed. A swift check confirmed that the chest of drawers and bedside cabinet were also empty. He must have taken his things into the spare bedroom. With some relief she stripped off her swimsuit, put on a brown terry bathrobe and went to the bathroom.

For half an hour she just lay in the bath and soaked and took her time drying and powdering herself, enjoying the ordinariness of the task. As she stepped out of the bathroom into the corridor Bruce poked his head round the kitchen door.

'Dinner in half an hour.' He eyed her appraisingly and Felicity hugged the bathrobe closer to her, conscious of her nakedness beneath it. He gave a thin smile and went back into the kitchen.

Dinner was a meat casserole with vegetables, served at a candlelit table.

'I thought you said you couldn't cook?' she remarked.

'I merely followed what it said in the book. It was really very simple.'

'It's very good.'

'Thank you. Perhaps I have hidden talents in that direction.'

'You seem to have hidden talents in many directions. As an amateur psychiatrist, for instance,' she said tartly, then bit her lip. 'I'm sorry, I shouldn't have said that.'

'No, you shouldn't.' But strangely enough he didn't sound angry. 'As a punishment you can do the washing-up.'

He wiped while she washed and it seemed so normal that Felicity wanted to scream. She couldn't go on pretending like this; she just couldn't. As soon as they were finished she said, 'I'm very tired. I'll go straight to bed.'

'Before you go, come into the sitting-room for a moment, will you? There's something I want to show you.'

Reluctantly she followed him to where he stood in the centre of the room. He took a long, thin black box from his jacket pocket. 'I intended to give you this last night, but things didn't turn out quite as I planned.' His mouth was wry as he snapped open the case.

Felicity found herself staring mesmerised at a pendant necklace set with diamonds and emeralds against the black velvet of the box. Her mouth felt suddenly dry and she took a step away from Bruce, her eyes went fleetingly to meet his and then quickly away. 'I can't take it. You know I can't.'

'It's a wedding present.'

'That doesn't make any difference. Bruce, please, you know I can't take it.'

'Why not, Felicity?'

'Because ... because ...' she floundered, unable to answer.

'Because you think I'm trying to buy you, is that it?'

'Yes, if you must know, that's exactly it.'

'Don't you know that a man is allowed to buy presents for his wife? Some women even seem to like it. And you are my wife, aren't you, Felicity?' he demanded, his voice imperative.

Slowly she nodded.

'Say it,' he commanded.

'Y-yes,' she whispered, afraid of antagonising him further.

'Then you must take the necklace.'

Felicity held out her hand for the case, but he said, 'I'll put it on for you,' and held the necklace waiting for her to come to him.

Hesitantly she did so and turned her back towards him so that he could fasten it. She found herself looking into a mirror on the wall and could see the pendant sparkling on the dark background of her dress where it hung between her breasts. Raising her wide, tension-racked eyes, she saw that Bruce was looking at her reflection too, a strange glint in his dark grey eyes. Deliberately he put his hands on her shoulders and she could feel them strong as steel through her dress. The familiar tremors of emotion began to course through her and suddenly she couldn't stand his nearness any longer.

Wrenching herself away from him, she tugged violently at the pendant until the delicate chain snapped and then she threw it at him with all her strength. It hit him on the chest. He made no attempt to catch it but let it fall at his feet unheeded.

'Don't ever touch me again! I hate it when you touch me, do you understand?' she cried fiercely. 'I'm not your wife and I never will be!' Then she turned and ran into her bedroom, locking the door behind her.

It was almost nine o'clock the next morning when Felicity awoke feeling stiff and languid, having slept very little during the night. For a long time she had sat fully dressed in the dark room, afraid of what Bruce might do, but she had heard him use the shower and then the sound of the other bedroom door being shut decisively.

When she went into the kitchen there were signs that he had already breakfasted, so she made herself toast and coffee and carried them on to the terrace. The sun was well up in the sky. It blazed down unhindered by the little bundles of cumulus cloud which hung motionless against the aquamarine of the sky. These first few hours were the best of the day. The sun licked the foliage clean of dew and sucked the dampness from the small breeze. Soon the moisture would congregate again to produce the heavy, humid air of midday.

Tired of the silence all around her, Felicity went to turn on the portable radio, but found that it wouldn't work.

Bruce walked up as she was fiddling with it. 'I'm afraid the batteries seem to be dead,' he said.

'Are there any spares?'

'I've looked around but can't find any. We'll have to make do with the radio on the boat. Was there something you particularly wanted to listen to?'

'No, I just felt like having some background music,' she said almost defensively.

'I see.' He sat down opposite her and lit a cigarette, looking away from her across the bay. His tones had been formal, very polite, as if he were speaking to someone he didn't know very well. Felicity had finished her breakfast before he spoke again. 'There's supposed to be an old wreck on the north side of the lagoon. I thought of going down to search for her this morning. Would you care to come along?'

Ordinarily Felicity would have jumped at the chance as she had never explored a sunken wreck before, but now she said hastily, 'I think I'll just sit by the pool and read.'

'As you wish.' His face and voice were expressionless, completely non-committal. He finished his cigarette before unhurriedly collecting his diving gear and going off to the far end of the lagoon.

Her book was the latest thriller by a best-selling author and one that she had been looking forward to reading, but Felicity found that she couldn't concentrate. Eventually she gave up trying and dived into the swimming pool. She lost count of the number of lengths she swam before she got too tired to go on, then she turned on to her back and floated, wondering if Bruce had found the wreck and what it was like. If it had been a sailing ship there might be cannons still lying there, she thought, wishing that she could see them. Perhaps she could go down alone and search when Bruce was out of the way.

At one o'clock she went into the house and prepared herself a tossed salad, leaving half in the fridge for Bruce. By two o'clock she could contain her curiosity no longer and began to stroll along the beach towards the northern end. His discarded clothing was piled neatly in the shade of a rock, but of Bruce there was no sign. Looking out over the gently waving waters of the lagoon, Felicity sought the telltale trail of bubbles that would give away his position, but she could see nothing.

Uneasily she looked back at his folded shirt and shorts, wondering how long he had been down. She remembered David's voice when he had warned her never to go diving alone for fear of accidents; but she had let Bruce go alone because she was afraid to be near him. Perhaps he had got trapped in the wreck and couldn't get up again! If she ran back to the bungalow she could get her set of tanks and go after him, but it was so far, nearly a mile away. She had begun to run when she remembered that the boat was nearer and that there was a spare set on board. But Bruce had probably locked the boat up; she daren't take the risk of getting to it and finding it locked. Quickly she ran back to his clothes and began to search feverishly in his pockets for the keys, panic making her fumble as she tried to hurry.

'You're wasting your time. It isn't there.'

Felicity turned to see Bruce wading out of the water on a line some distance from where she had looked for him. She felt such a wave of relief at seeing him that she hardly heard what he had said.

'Did you really think I would be stupid enough to leave the key lying there for you to take? I had an idea you'd be down here searching for it the moment my back was turned.'

Felicity stared at him dumbly. It hadn't even occurred to her to try to get away in the boat. 'I—I wasn't ...' Her voice trailed away beneath his scorn.

'Weren't you? What were you looking for then?'

'It's true I was looking for the keys, but not for the reason you think. I wanted to get something from the boat.'

'What was it?'

She shook her head. 'It doesn't matter now.'

He looked at her derisively and began to take off the heavy tanks.

'Did you find the wreck?' she asked tentatively.

'Yes, she must have been down there about a hundred and fifty years, I should think. That last hurricane must have shifted her a bit; there are one or two interesting things lying around.'

Felicity was silent, remembering that last hurricane all too vividly. Perhaps he was too, for he said more gently, 'I'll recharge the tanks and go down again tomorrow.' He hadn't looked at her, but Felicity knew he was giving her another opportunity.

Casually she said, 'Perhaps I'd better come with you. It isn't really safe to dive alone.'

'The wreck isn't dangerous as long as you take care. It's too broken up.'

Bruce collected his gear and they walked back to the house, together but apart.

This formal manner, as if they were polite strangers, carried Felicity through the rest of the day until she could escape to her room, but the next morning he took her down to the wreck and she was able to relax as they searched among the broken spars and timbers. By brushing gently away at the sand they found two coins, but Felicity, although fascinated by it, found the old wreck strangely depressing and was glad to return to the warmth and light when Bruce touched her arm and pointed to the surface.

Back on the beach Felicity examined their finds excitedly. 'Are they gold coins? Do you think they're valuable?'

Bruce carefully broke off the encrustations that had grown on them during their long sojourn in the sea. 'This one could be, but I think the other is silver. Colin Marsh is quite an expert on old coins. We can take them along to him when we get back and get him to clean them up for us.'

The excitement over the find was suddenly gone; Felicity didn't want to think about going back to Trenaka; she didn't want to think of the future at all.

She never quite knew how she got through the next few days. Afraid always to relax her ground, she couldn't enjoy anything they did together, but became oddly restless when by herself. One morning they picked their way over the rocks to reach a strip of sand bordering the sea. There was only an occasional puff of wind to temper the blazing sun and ruffle the water. The sea was jade green over the shallows, broken by tints of gold and orange where the coral reached near the surface and caught the sunlight. Farther out the water shaded to topaz, then, towards the horizon, the dense blue of sapphire. Bruce chose a suitable rock and clipped together his fishing rod.

'This should be a good place to catch yellow-tails,' he told her.

'It looks very difficult,' Felicity observed as she watched him send the line spinning effortlessly into a deep pool between the rocks.

'It's easy enough when you get the hang of it. Here, I'll show you.' Carefully he demonstrated before letting her take the rod, but Felicity found it awkward to control without fouling up the line. After a few attempts she gave up and let him take the rod back and he soon caught two fish which he put in a keep net.

'Have another try,' he encouraged her.

Again Felicity took the line, but without much success.

'Look, like this.' He came behind her and reached out to put his hands over hers, then swung back and forwards again so that the float landed exactly where he wanted it. Felicity had stiffened beneath his touch, but he stood away immediately and became polite and impersonal again. Eventually she got the hang of it and managed to catch a fish. Bruce hooked them all together and carried them back to the beach where he collected the dead wood he found on the tide line and built a fire in a pit in the sand.

'What are you doing?' Felicity asked curiously.

'Cooking our lunch.' Deftly he cleaned the fish and then rolled them up in wild banana leaves. When the flames had died down he buried the fish in the hot ashes of the fire. 'They'll be cooked through soon.'

They ate the fish with their fingers and Felicity found them delicious. For a dessert Bruce broke open a coconut on a sharp stone and gave her the sweet milk to drink.

'Mm,' she licked her fingers like a child. 'That was fun!'

'We could have lots more fun, if you could only relax a little, Felicity,' he said softly.

Immediately she felt the tension returning and looked away. 'I think I'll go for a swim.'

'You'd better wait a few minutes. You could get cramp if you swim straight after a meal.' His voice was coldly polite again.

On their fifth evening at Jabalya Key they had dined together as usual, sitting at each end of a long table and making 'pass the salt' type remarks. Afterwards Felicity had cleared but refused Bruce's offer of help to wash the dishes. Finding her novel that she had been trying to read, she settled down in an armchair by the window. Bruce was studying some old charts he had found in a cupboard, but presently he rose and selected a record to put on the stereo record player. The haunting music of Rachmaninov's Variations on a Theme of Paganini filled the room, her ears and her heart. She felt a deep longing within her, but didn't know what it was for. Abruptly she stood up, intending to go to her room, but Bruce, too, had risen to his feet and barred her way.

'Would you like to dance?' He held out his arms.

'N-no, of course not.'

She went to push past him, but he said softly, 'Little coward.'

Her chin came up and she stood facing him for a moment before defiantly letting him put his arms around her. She had expected to feel nervous, but she found the warmth of his arms strangely comforting. The frustrated yearning was gone as he guided her slowly round the furniture. Was this what she wanted? Was this what she longed for? The enormity of the thought made her suddenly stand stock still, then she tore herself from his grasp and ran to switch off the music.

Startled, Bruce had to let her go and Felicity turned to

face him as, ashen-faced and trembling, she leant against the stereo for support. 'I can't stand any more of this, do you hear me? I can't stay here alone with you any longer!' Her voice had risen and she was almost shouting at him, her nerves cracking at last under the intolerable strain.

'Felicity, for heaven's sake calm down. I'm not an ogre who's going to pounce on you at any moment. If you'll only give it time we can ...'

'No! You've got to take me back to Trenaka! Can't you see that I can't stand being shut away with you any more? It's like a nightmare that goes on and on ...' She buried her face in her hands and shook with emotion.

He studied her intently, his mouth taut. 'You realise that if we go back so soon there'll be a great deal of gossip? It won't be pleasant, Felicity.'

'Pleasant! Do you think I care about that! I just want to get away from here—away from you!'

His eyes blazed and Felicity was afraid he was going to take hold of her. She shrank away from him.

'Very well,' he said tightly. 'We'll leave for Trenaka in the morning.' Then he turned away and left her standing alone.

But there was to be no gossip in Trenaka about their early return, for just after dawn the next morning they heard the sound of a boat's siren in the lagoon. Running to the window, Felicity was amazed to see the hospital motor boat pulling up to the jetty. Hastily she began to dress, but found that Bruce was before her and was already standing on the jetty talking to Joey when she got there. Joey looked at her unhappily, the usual cheery grin completely gone from his face.

'I'm really sorry to spoil your holiday, doctor, and Dr Mac, he's sorry as well.'

Puzzled Felicity looked from Joey to Bruce and saw that he, too, looked worried. 'What is it?' she asked anxiously.

Bruce held out a letter. 'It's from Mac. Evidently a 'flu epidemic has started on the islands. It appears to be a particularly virulent form that can prove fatal for anyone who isn't strong enough to fight it. He tried to contact us by radio, but of course ours wasn't working.'

Felicity read the brief letter apologising for breaking up her honeymoon but asking her to return to help look after the critically ill.

'You'd better leave at once,' she heard Bruce say. 'It will be quicker if you go back with Joey in the motor boat. I'll clear up here and join you as soon as I can.'

'Yes—yes, I suppose that would be best.' Felicity stole a quick glance at him, but his face was impassive. Joey helped her down into the boat and Bruce cast off.

'Be seeing you,' he said casually. As casually as he would have said it to someone he hadn't seen for years and never expected to see again.

CHAPTER EIGHT

THE 'flu epidemic had spread not only through Trenaka but also to some of the outlying islands, and Mac, with the help of his medical staff, was trying desperately to contain it within this area. The virus was of the Asian type and particularly lethal to the native Amerindians, who had no inborn resistance to it as the European community had. Mac put Felicity in charge of the hospital while he and Geoff ranged themselves over the whole area, giving their limited and precious 'flu vaccine injections only to the old and the weak, bringing in the very sick and organising their resources as best they could until the epidemic wore itself out.

Felicity realised with relief that she would have to live at the hospital for the time being and asked Ellen, who was helping there, to let Bruce know. On the first evening when she finally managed to snatch some rest, she found the suitcase that she had taken to Jabalya Key waiting for her in the room set aside for her use, the clothes neatly packed inside. She let her fingers run over them for a moment and then quickly extracted her nightdress. There was no time for thinking; there was too much work to be done.

For days Felicity had not seen Bruce but had spoken to him on the telephone in his official capacity, asking him for urgently needed supplies to be flown out from America, to organise a temporary ward and more beds for the increasing number of patients, and to arrange funerals for those who died penniless and alone. Everything she asked for and more besides, he did with extreme efficiency, trying to ease the burden on the three doctors by taking as much on his shoulders and those of the other officials as he possibly could.

The epidemic was still raging, but they had reason to be hopeful that they had broken its back when, over a week later, Bruce came to the hospital. He had called before, but luckily Felicity had always been busy with a patient and hadn't seen him, but now she was standing in the vestibule with Edwina, trying to work out where to put two more urgent cases.

'You'd better put them in the room I've been using,' Felicity was saying. 'I can manage quite easily on the couch in the office.'

'I don't think that's a good idea at all,' Bruce said as he came up to them.

Felicity turned reluctantly to face him and his mouth tightened when he saw her eyes, deep-shadowed by tiredness.

'I thought as much. You haven't been sleeping, or eating properly either, from the look of you. Edwina, I'm taking my wife out for a meal. Can you cope for an hour or so?'

'Bruce, I can't leave here now! Don't you realise that . . .'

'I realise that if you don't get away from here for a while you'll crack up. Well, Edwina?'

The other girl smiled. 'Of course we can cope. Just leave a number in case of emergency.'

Felicity found herself helped out of her white coat and bundled into the car. Bruce drove to a quiet restaurant where a table was immediately found for him. The waiter brought platefuls of delicate hors d'oeuvres which Felicity bit into hungrily, only now aware of how she had skimped her food during the hectic days of the last week. Bruce didn't try to talk to her, merely letting her eat her fill and replenishing her glass with wine.

'Thank you,' she said at last. 'I didn't realise how much I needed that.'

'Doctors are all the same, they never look after themselves properly.'

'I really ought to get back now.'

'We'll walk down to the harbour first. Some fresh air will do you good.'

Felicity made a half-hearted protest, but he wouldn't listen, instead taking her elbow and guiding her down the street to the harbour wall. A light breeze ruffled her hair and she became aware that it was hastily tied back with an elastic band, and that she was still wearing the flat, serviceable working shoes that made Bruce seem so much taller even than before.

'I must look a mess,' she said, trying to push her hair back in place.

He smiled. 'The meal must have done you good if you're starting to worry about your appearance!' Leaning against the wall, he lit cigarettes for them both and handed one to her. Felicity had read somewhere that this gesture was like a kiss. But it wasn't, definitely not.

'Mac tells me he thinks he can see an end to the epidemic.'

'Yes, I think the worst is over. We still have lots of very sick patients and more coming in, but the number contracting the virus is beginning to fall.'

'How soon do you think you'll be able to come home?'

'Home?' For a moment she didn't understand what he meant.

'Yes, home! To my house, the house we intended to live in until the new one on the hill was built, remember?' His tone had hardened slightly.

'I—I don't know. I haven't had time to think about that.'

'Then give it some thought, will you? There are some things we have to get straight between us. Will you do that?' He looked at her searchingly and Felicity nodded wordlessly. Apparently satisfied, he led her to the car and drove back to the hospital. 'Be sure you get some rest,' he admonished her.

'Yes. Thank you for the meal.'

Gradually the number of emergency cases coming in lessened, although Mac and Geoff were still away, only returning to the hospital from time to time to collect supplies or bring in new patients. All of them were extremely weary but pleased that the epidemic seemed to be on the wane. Bruce's intervention in stopping all inter-island travel had certainly helped to contain it in the one area.

The outing with Bruce had done her good for only a short time, for soon Felicity was eating only quick snacks and she had, of course, given up her room to the patients, taking short, often interrupted, naps on the couch whenever she could spare the time, which, as she was extremely conscientious, wasn't often. During the whole of one long hot afternoon and evening she fought hard for the life of a woman already weak from the birth of a child, but the 'flu virus had taken too strong a hold before the woman was brought in and Felicity was unable to save her. Wearily she pulled off the surgical mask she was wearing and braced herself to tell the dead woman's family, who were waiting with large anxious eyes, hoping that the lady doctor had performed a miracle.

Felicity looked at them, her throat dry. How she hated moments like this, but they had to be faced. 'I'm sorry. There was nothing we could do.'

The women began to cry, loud wailing sobs that went right through her aching head, but the woman's husband just stood there, looking at her with hatred in his eyes because she was no goddess, no performer of miracles, after all. She found that she couldn't bear his look and turned to go in the grounds for some fresh, cooling air. Her feet dragged with tiredness so that she stumbled over a step and fell, grazing her knees.

A little exclamation of pain escaped her and wearily she tried to drag herself to her feet, but then there were strong arms lifting her, picking her up. She was aware of the lean strength of Bruce's body, of his clean, masculine smell.

Curiously she didn't want to get away; she wanted only to nestle here in his arms and be nursed like a child. But that wouldn't do; he was her enemy and she must fight him till the end. Weakly she began to struggle, but he only held her tighter and said, 'Be still, little one. Don't you know when you're beaten?'

Indistinctly she heard him talking to someone on the telephone. Then he picked her up again from the couch where he had set her down, and putting her in his car, drove along the darkened streets. Pulling up at his house, he carried her inside and up the stairs to a bedroom. Felicity's head was swimming with exhaustion and the pain from her knees, but she knew where she was and she began to fight in earnest now, trying to get away from him and out of the door. Easily, almost casually, he caught her wrists and held her prisoner. He looked down at her with sudden heat in his eyes and Felicity tensed beneath his hands.

Then there was a sound in the doorway and he turned away, his face expressionless again. 'Here she is, Ellen—still fighting to get back to the hospital. Make her see some sense, will you, and put her to bed? I must arrange for Geoff to take over until she's rested.'

Ellen came and took Felicity from him, her hands gentle, her soothing words a lullaby, and Felicity found herself being undressed, her injured knees cleaned, and helped into a large double bed, its softness and crisp white sheets a welcome delight after the hardness of the office couch. Even as Ellen smoothed the covers over her she fell into a deep exhausted sleep.

When Felicity finally awoke to find that she had slept the clock round, she felt terribly guilty and wanted to get back to the hospital straight away, but Ellen refused to let her.

'Bruce will skin me alive if I even let you put your feet on the floor. He left strict instructions that you were to stay in bed all day and not go back to the hospital until

140

tomorrow.' Ellen looked at her compassionately. 'You poor bairn, you've been working yourself to a standstill for the last two weeks.'

'But you've been working there, too, Ellen.'

'Yes, but I wasn't just getting used to being married, with all the physical and emotional adjustments that entails, *and* I went home at night. It's a wonder that you've lasted out so long. Now you lie back and I'll send Jemima up with some lunch. And you be sure to eat it, now. I'll look in on you again later this afternoon.'

'Yes, Ellen,' Felicity said meekly, as the older woman plumped up her pillows and then gave her a quick hug.

'Poor lassie! It's been a bad start to your married life, but we must see that you and Bruce are together again soon.'

Ellen had meant the words to be comforting, but Felicity was acutely aware that the time would soon come when she would no longer have an excuse to live at the hospital, but fortunately she was still needed there for the time being. So she was completely unprepared for Bruce's announcement when he came home that evening.

She had found that Jemima, the female half of the married couple Bruce employed, had put away all the clothes that she hadn't taken on honeymoon in the various drawers and wardrobes, so she was able to wash her hair and change into a dress. It was pleasant to feel feminine again and to be able to sit in the garden and rest before dinner. After over two weeks cooped up in the hospital it was heaven to smell the heady scents of the bougainvillea and oleander flowers; rather like sitting in a tropical nursery, she thought dreamily.

Bruce came to find her when he came home and joined her on the seat. 'How do you feel?' he asked.

'Much better, thank you. I shall be ready to go back to the hospital after dinner.'

He drew on his cigarette. 'I've been talking to Mac about that. We've arranged for Geoff to take over from you at night so that you can come home and get some sleep.'

'Well, you can just unarrange it!' There were bright sparks of anger in Felicity's eyes. 'Until the crisis is over and my services are no longer required, I shall continue to live at the hospital.'

'The epidemic is dying out and both Mac and Geoff will now have more time to spend here in Trenaka. It's only reasonable that they should take some of the burden from you.'

'But Geoff will still be working day and night, and if he is then I must too. I don't want any concessions because I'm a woman.'

'Don't be a little fool. You don't have the strength of a man. You've driven yourself beyond the point of exhaustion already, not to mention the fact that you were cracking up with nervous tension before we left Jabalya Key. I've told Mac that you'll be coming here at nights, and that's final!'

'I see.' Felicity stood facing him, seething with fury. 'You *told* Mac! So I'm to be given preferential treatment, not because I'm a woman, but because I happen to be married to you! And as you're the senior officer your orders have to be obeyed. But not by me! I shall continue to live at the hospital!'

She went to walk back to the house, but as she passed he caught her wrist. Vainly she tried to pull away, but his fingers were like steel and she stopped, bristling with resentment.

'Why don't you admit the real reason for wanting to live at the hospital, Felicity? Why not tell the truth and say that you're afraid to live in the same house with me; afraid to stop fighting me and let your heart take over from your mind? For God's sake grow up! You're a woman now, not a fifteen-year-old schoolgirl!' He paused, but she said nothing. Almost derisively he let go of her wrist. 'You should know by now that you have nothing to fear from me. I'm not the type who goes around forcing himself on unwilling females—even if the female in question does happen to be my wife! But don't try me too far, because I'm flesh and blood the same as the next man. You're too tired now to talk this thing through, but sooner or later you've got to face up to the fact that we're married and that we've got to live with each other. And to do that you have to trust me—completely!' He stood there, his hands clenched at his sides, his chin aggressive; a man of tremendous will who would not for long be denied if she continued to resist him.

Luckily, Jemima's husband, Albert, came to tell them that dinner was ready, so she could safely turn and hurry back to the house. During the meal Bruce brought her up to date on events on the islands, but she wasn't concentrating and answered only in monosyllables, so that he eventually lapsed into silence. Immediately after the meal she excused herself on the grounds of tiredness.

Bruce escorted her to the door. 'I'll run you to the hospital in the morning and pick you up about six in the evening.'

Felicity opened her mouth to protest, then stayed silent, knowing that it was useless.

As she turned to go up the stairs, he added, 'And you needn't bother to lock your door tonight. We don't have pirates any more on Trenaka.'

Their lives began to fall into a pattern. Bruce would take her to the hospital in the mornings and collect her later in the evening, except for two nights a week when she worked late so that Geoff could have some time off. Geoff didn't tell her where he went on these occasions and she didn't ask, but she assumed that he was seeing Gillian, and was worried, because she liked her colleague and was afraid that the affair might come out into the open with the ensuing scandal bringing unhappiness to all three sides of the triangle. Their own relationship was no longer as friendly as before, but they had their work in common and there was no antagonism between them.

Not as there was between herself and Bruce. The two of them would be coolly polite to one another over dinner and then Bruce would go to his study to work, or Felicity to her room. It was as if a high, insurmountable wall was being built between them, one that grew higher with every day that passed. But Bruce wasn't the man to let the situation go on indefinitely, she knew. One day he would break down the wall whether she liked it or not. So she must think again of some way of destroying him before that day came.

When the epidemic was almost over and most of the patients well on their road to recovery, Felicity and Bruce received an invitation to a reception at the Residency for some visiting dignitary. Bruce, as senior officer, was, of course, expected to attend, and the invitation included Felicity.

'They don't really want me,' she said when she read it. 'No one will mind if you go alone.' By 'no one' she meant Sir Miles and Lady Steventon, whom she hadn't seen since the wedding.

'On the contrary,' Bruce contradicted her. 'We've been asked to attend as a married couple and we shall go in that style.' His eyes held hers compellingly. 'Do you understand me, Felicity? We're going as a newly and happily married man and woman, not as two people who can hardly tolerate the sight of each other. Is that quite clear?'

'Oh, it's clear all right. You couldn't have explained more explicitly that your career comes first and that not a breath of scandal is going to be allowed to harm it. We may both have to live a lie, but that doesn't matter so long as the great Bruce Gresham gets to the top!' Felicity turned away bitterly, but Bruce's next words stopped her cold.

'You can't bury your head in the sand for ever, Felicity. I've already suggested to Sir Miles that in a month or so I'd like to take another leave to finish our interrupted honeymoon. And this time it *will* be a honeymoon!' he added grimly.

Completely unable to answer, Felicity hurried to her room and subsided on the bed. She would have to do something soon, she thought dully. It was impossible now to create the type of scandal that would have been caused if she had run away from him. Having to come back to Trenaka because of the epidemic had ruined all chances of that, and she hadn't been able to think of anything else that would be half so effective. Slowly she looked down at the invitation still clutched in her hand. Unless—an idea gradually formed in her mind. Suppose she took the opportunity of the reception to talk to Lady Steventon—tell her that the marriage hadn't been consummated—that it was all a mistake? Cecily Steventon hadn't wanted her to marry Bruce, but if she appealed to her as a woman? Asked her to help her to get an annulment? The scandal *that* would arouse in Government circles would be even juicier than a divorce!

The more she thought about it, the better she liked the idea. She would have to discreetly put the blame for the failure on Bruce, of course, but that shouldn't be difficult. After all, there hadn't been any witnesses, she thought cynically. And if Bruce used her made-up story as an excuse, then she would simply deny it.

It was half-way through the evening before Felicity had an opportunity to get Lady Steventon alone for a moment. 'Lady Steventon, could I speak to you, please?' Bruce was showing the visiting dignitary's wife round the picture gallery and Felicity was afraid that he might come back at any moment, although the lady had been so captivated by his charm that she might keep him to herself for some time, with any luck.

'Of course,' her hostess replied. 'This is your first reception, isn't it? Are you enjoying yourself?'

'Yes, thank you. But I—I rather wanted to speak to you

privately,' Felicity said, with a hurried look in the direction of the gallery.

The older woman looked at her, seeing her eyes, dark pools of tension in her pale face. 'Very well, come to my sitting-room for a moment.'

Thankfully Felicity followed her, mentally rehearsing all the things she must say. Once inside the sitting-room with the door firmly shut, she began, 'Lady Steventon, this is rather difficult for me to say, but . . .'

But Lady Steventon held up a restraining hand. 'But you don't have to. I know exactly what you're going to ask.'

'Y-you do?' Felicity stared, completely taken aback.

'Yes. Both Sir Miles and Bruce have told me how hard you've been working, and I assure you that it needs no intervention from me to persuade Sir Miles to let you both have leave so that you can finish your honeymoon just as soon as you can be spared. I know how unhappy it must have made you both to have to come back so soon.'

Felicity gazed at her in consternation. 'But—but that wasn't . . .'

'My dear,' Lady Steventon refused to be interrupted, 'I'm rather ashamed to say that I was extremely disappointed when you and Bruce became engaged. I didn't think that you were the right woman for him and I had hoped that . . . But that doesn't matter now. What I wanted to tell you, Felicity,' she said, using her given name for the first time, 'was that your selfless work at the hospital during the epidemic, putting the islanders before your marriage, has made me realise all the qualities that Bruce first saw in you—your kindness and courage, your dedication and unselfishness.' She reached out and took Felicity's slack hand in hers. 'I hope, my dear, that in future we will be better friends. And I want you to promise me that if ever you need help or advice you won't hesitate to come to me. Will you do that?'

For a moment Felicity stared at her speechlessly, completely put out by Lady Steventon's change of heart. 'Y—yes,' she faltered, and gathered herself to deliver her set speech. 'As a matter of fact, there was some ...' But she broke off as there was a sharp rap on the door and it was immediately opened. Bruce stood in the doorway.

Felicity felt herself going scarlet and hastily turned her face away. But he had seen, and noticed also how she had hastily removed her hand from Cecily Steventon's.

His eyes were like steel, but he smiled charmingly as he came up behind her and put his hands on her shoulders, gripping so hard that she nearly winced aloud. 'What has Felicity been telling you?' he asked nonchalantly, his voice like silk. 'You mustn't let her keep you from your guests, Cecily.'

Lady Steventon smiled at them, seeing nothing but a possessive bridegroom. 'On the contrary, Felicity has hardly been able to say a word. I've already told her that you will be able to get away together before very long. Was there anything else you wanted to ask me, Felicity?'

The grip on her shoulders tightened fiercely. 'N-no, thank you.'

'Then I'll rejoin the others. Don't keep Felicity up too late, Bruce, she still looks very tired.'

Bruce opened the door for her and Felicity put up a hand to rub her bruised shoulder.

'Why did you get Cecily alone? Just what are you trying to pull?' His voice was savage.

'Nothing. I'd like to go back to the house now, please.'

'Not until you tell me the truth.'

'There's nothing to tell; she just said she hoped we'd be better friends.'

'But you were going to tell her about us, weren't you?' Felicity went to turn away, but he swung her round to face him. 'Weren't you?'

'All right, yes! If you must know,' she shouted angrily. 'I wanted her to help me get away from you. I can't stand any more of this—this fiasco. I want an annulment!'

He stared at her, his eyes blazing, his lips set in a thin hard line, and Felicity was suddenly afraid she'd gone too far. But his expression changed to one of disgust. 'You're an even bigger coward than I thought. You haven't even given us a chance to work things out. You're so afraid of facing up to things that you just want to run away and pretend that nothing has happened. But you're going to face up to them, and if you ever try to pull anything like this again ...' He saw the look of defiance in her eyes as she thought that he couldn't stop her. Silkily he added, 'Then I'll just have to make sure that you have nothing to tell, won't I?'

Felicity stared at him, completely shattered by his words. So he would take even that weapon away from her? Tears of despair glistened on her lashes and she hurriedly turned away from him. She wouldn't let him see that he had beaten her, she wouldn't!

'Telephone call for you, Felicity,' Edwina told her as she was passing her desk the next morning.

'Thanks, I'll take it in the office. Hallo, Dr Lambert speaking.'

'Dr Lambert? What happened to your married name? Or did you forget?' Felicity recognised Gillian's voice.

'No, I didn't forget. I find it more convenient to use my maiden name when I'm working; it's easier for the staff,' she told Gillian. But it wasn't true; merely an excuse. How could she use Bruce's name when she wasn't truly his wife, or ever would be? 'What can I do for you, Gillian?' she asked, pushing the thought from her mind.

'I heard you were back in the social whirl, so I wondered if you'd like to come swimming this afternoon. We could go to that little beach we went to before and laze around.'

'This afternoon? I'm awfully tired, Gillian, would you mind if I ...?'

'Please don't say no,' Gillian broke in. 'I'm bored to tears and there's been no one to talk to except the Service

148

wives, and they're forever trying to give me good advice, so do say you'll come. At least you don't try to lecture me all the time.'

Felicity laughed. 'I'm highly flattered. All right, Gillian, I'll come. Where shall I meet you?'

'I'll pick you up at your place at two. Thanks, Felicity. See you later.'

The sea was cool and refreshing after the heat of the town and Felicity floated on her back for a long time, too tired to make the effort to swim properly. She became aware that Gillian was calling to her and reluctantly turned to go back to the beach.

'I was beginning to be afraid you'd fallen asleep,' Gillian said.

'I must admit I feel terribly lethargic today—I can't think why. The hospital's almost back to normal now.'

'Can't you? I can. It's something that most newly married couples experience quite frequently,' Gillian said, looking at her rather archly.

'Oh!' Felicity flushed as she caught the nuance of the remark.

The older girl laughed. 'All right, I won't tease.' Stretching out on her beach mat, she went on, 'It's a great shame that you had to give up your honeymoon, though. I bet Bruce was absolutely furious.'

'Just one of the perils of being a doctor,' Felicity said lightly.

'Never mind, I hear the Steventons are arranging another leave for you so that you can continue where you left off. But it won't be the same.'

'No,' Felicity said shortly. 'It couldn't be the same. How's Colin?' she asked, to change the subject.

'All right, I suppose. He said he might drop by later. He and David are going to look at a forestry site that's being cleared on the western ridge and they have to pass this way on their way back.'

If Felicity was surprised she tried not to show it. Usually

Gillian was rather scathing about Colin and she had never asked him to join them for a swim before. Did it mean that she was growing tired of Geoff? Felicity certainly hoped so.

The men came about an hour later and immediately went in for a swim with Gillian, while Felicity stayed on the beach, feeling too tired to move. Soon David came to drop down beside her, sprinkling not unwelcome drops of sea-water on her hot body.

'Glad to see you taking a break,' he said. 'This epidemic must have taken a lot out of you. You looked pretty fagged.'

'Thanks,' Felicity said wryly. 'It's nice to see you again, too.'

David grinned his open, friendly smile. 'I always say the wrong things to you, don't I?' he said ruefully. 'I wish I didn't, then maybe I'd be married to you now instead of Bruce.'

Felicity looked up at him expecting to join in the joke, but one look at David's serious, wistful eyes and she knew that it was no joke! Fortunately Colin chased Gillian up the beach to join them then, and the next minute they were all laughing together, the incident temporarily buried.

Colin was demanding food and Gillian distributed the picnic she had brought. They seemed happy together, Felicity thought, and watching them felt a stab of envy. Then she noticed that David was looking at her and she hastily joined in the jokes and laughter.

'By the way,' David remarked before they left, 'I've got a present for you. I'll drop round with it some time.' The two men drove away, leaving the girls to have a last swim, but as they carried their things towards the car, Gillian gave a cry of pain.

'My foot! I must have trodden on some glass or something.' She sat down and bent to peer at her left foot.

'Here, let me look.' Felicity dropped to her knees beside her. 'It doesn't look like a cut, there isn't any blood. Oh, here it is! It looks like a thorn, but it must have gone in pretty deeply.'

'No, look!' Gillian had been scrabbling about in the sand with her hands and now showed Felicity a spiky marine creature she had dug up. 'It's a sea-urchin. Their thorns are dreadful if you tread on them. You can't even walk on the foot for ages unless they're drawn out straight away. Can't you get it out for me, Felicity?'

'I haven't anything here. I'd have to take you back to the hospital.'

'Please. I don't want to be laid up now. I was going out tonight.'

Tonight being Geoff's night off, Felicity thought. It seemed that she had been wrong in thinking that Gillian had tired of Geoff, after all. As it happened he was just going into the hospital as they arrived, and gave Gillian a helping arm into the surgery. Gillian immediately began to chat animatedly to him, so Felicity decided she was *de trop* and left Geoff to extract the thorn. Sitting down at her desk, she began to write up some case notes when Geoff looked in to say that he would run Gillian home.

'Have a good evening,' Felicity said mildly.

He gave her a sardonic look but said nothing. The evening at the hospital passed quietly enough and Felicity decided to catch up at last on some paper-work and reading that had been neglected during the worst of the epidemic. At about ten-thirty a young student nurse came to tell her that a patient had been brought into Casualty. Felicity rose at once, but her legs felt like lead beneath her. She shook her head in an effort to wake herself up, realising that she had been almost asleep in her chair. This wouldn't do. Crossing to the drug cupboard, she took out two benzedrine tablets and swallowed them with a glass of water, then hurried after the nurse.

The patient was sprawled on the examination couch in a cubicle. He was a big, burly man dressed in rough working clothes, and Felicity guessed that he was a sailor from one

151

of the banana boats moored at the wharf. 'All right, nurse, I'll see to him, but send an orderly in as soon as possible, will you?'

As she bent to examine him she drew back distastefully; the man reeked of rum. There was a severe gash on his arm and she had to cut away the sleeve of his shirt in order to stitch and dress it. She gave a local anaesthetic, although the sailor snored in such a drunken stupor that it hardly seemed necessary. He must have been hardier than she thought, however, for after a while he began to come to and demanded to know what she was doing.

'Don't try to move. You have a bad cut on your arm.'

'What are you, a nurse?' The man's voice was thick and slurred with drink.

'No, I'm a doctor. You're at Trenaka hospital.'

'A doctor, eh?' He eyed her up and down lasciviously, his every look an insult. 'I shall have to get myself cut up in a knife fight more often.'

'A knife fight? Was the other man hurt?'

'How the hell should I know? He's probably at the bottom of the harbour by now.' He leered at her. 'What's your name?'

Hastily Felicity finished taping the bandage, wondering where on earth the orderly had got to. 'There, you can go now. And if the other man was hurt make sure he comes in for treatment.' She turned to put the instruments she had used to be sterilised, but found to her horror that the sailor had come up behind her and put his arms round her. Angrily she turned in his arms, intending to push him away, but that was a mistake, for it brought her face near to his and he immediately tried to kiss her, his bearded mouth with the blackened teeth seeking hers.

He was a big brute of a man and Felicity knew herself to be no match for him. Urgently she yelled for help, but the other night staff couldn't have been within hearing, because no one came. His hairy, dirty hands were stroking her now and, utterly revolted, Felicity screamed in good earnest.

'What's the matter? Don't you know a good man when you see one?' He tried to claw at her overall and undo the buttons, but Felicity managed to scratch his face. Angrily he shook her off, but as he did so someone caught his arm from behind and swung him round, away from her. There was a short, nasty scuffle and then the sailor swore horribly and made off into the night.

David crossed to where Felicity stood, white and shaking. 'Felicity, are you all right? Did that brute hurt you?'

'No, I—I'm all right—really. Oh, David, thank heaven you came along!' There was a distinct break in her voice.

'Here, sit down. You look frightened to death.' There was concern in his voice.

'I must admit I don't feel terribly bright.' Shakily she sat down on the hard chair while David brought her a glass of water.

'Are you sure you're okay, Felicity? Would you like me to take you home?'

'No, I'll be fine in a minute. Just shock, that's all.' Trying hard to pull herself together, she said rather jerkily, 'Were you going past or something? I must have screamed loud enough to rouse the town.'

'No, I was coming here, as a matter of fact. I'd just parked the car when I heard you, so I just dropped the present and started running.'

'P-present?' she queried.

'You remember this morning I told you I had a present for you? I thought I'd drop it in here, rather than go up to the house.'

'Yes, I see.' Nothing was said, but there was a tacit understanding that he hadn't wanted to see her with Bruce. 'What was it?'

'A pair of candlesticks that I fashioned out of some coral.'

'Thank you, that was k-kind of you.' Suddenly her hand was shaking so that she could no longer hold the glass. She rose to her feet intending to set it down, but her legs were so unsteady that she almost fell.

Quickly David took the glass and put an arm round her to support her. 'What is it? Are you ill?'

'Just terribly tired and hot. The heat this afternoon must have affected me.' She looked up at him, her eyes misty. 'I'm sorry to have given you so much trouble, David.'

His arms tightened. 'What's a best man for except to provide a shoulder for the bride to lean on?' He tried to speak lightly, but his voice was husky. 'Felicity, if you're ever in trouble; if you ever need a friend, just remember ...'

'Felicity doesn't need a friend. She has a husband!' Bruce's voice was clipped, ice-cold, behind them.

Quickly, guiltily, they drew apart and turned to stare at him. David opened his mouth to protest, but Bruce cut him short. 'Felicity, go and get in the car. Geoff is back and I'm taking you home.' He had given her one swift glance that left her feeling limp and frozen.

'Bruce, it isn't what you think.' Vainly she made an attempt to explain, but he was in no mood to listen.

'I told you to get in the car,' he commanded harshly, and she glimpsed the arrogance he could display.

She hesitated, but then took off her overall and slowly walked towards the door, a look of mute appeal in her eyes as she passed David.

What passed between them she didn't know, but Bruce joined her after a few minutes, his face a mask of anger, his eyes blazing. David's large American car was drawn up outside the main entrance and Bruce said contemptuously, 'David really should learn to get himself a less obtrusive car when he goes calling on other men's wives.'

Felicity didn't bother to argue with him. What would be the use? In his present mood he would never believe the truth. All she longed for was to get back to the house and shut herself in her room. Her head ached abominably and her whole body felt as if fiery needles were being pushed into her. She shut her eyes for a few moments, but everything began to swim and she hastily opened them again. Dully she realised that Bruce was driving up into the hills.

'Where are you taking me?' she asked.

'We're going somewhere where we can talk. I'm damned if I'll put up with this situation any longer!'

'I told you it wasn't what you think,' Felicity said desperately. 'There was a drunken sailor. He tried to attack me, but David came and chased him off.'

'How very gallant of David.' His tone was infinitely sarcastic. 'I suppose he just happened to be driving past?'

'Well, no, he ... he ...' She stopped miserably, knowing what he would say.

'Exactly!' His voice jeered at her. 'And just how often has David visited you when you were alone at the hospital?'

'This was the first time,' she said defensively.

'And the last! Or by God, I'll have David off the island by the next plane!'

He drew up with a jerk and roughly pulled Felicity out of the car after him. There was a bright full moon and she had no difficulty in knowing where she was. He had brought her to the house site on the side of the mountain. Taking her arm, he hurried her along the path, not bothering to slow down even when she dragged behind, almost running to keep up with him. At last he reached the clearing and swung her round to face him, his eyes dark with anger.

'All right, Felicity, just what was the big idea? To make me jealous; to turn another knife in the wound? Or did you want to find out what you missed by not marrying David? He would have suited you, wouldn't he? A gentle, complacent husband who would never make demands on you? Well, I'm making demands on you, Felicity. You're my wife, and I'm going to show you just what that means!'

Using the last of her strength, Felicity pulled away from him and tried to run, but he sprang after her and caught her, his face black with fury.

'Bruce, please let me go! Please! I feel so ill. Please take me back to the house.' Panic-stricken, she pleaded with him, her breath hot and rasping in her throat.

She tried to struggle against him, but he held her with contemptuous ease as one hand moved slowly across her shoulder to her neck, unbuttoning the top of her dress and sliding inside to grip her throat caressingly. Felicity tried to protest, but she found she couldn't speak, could only stare up at him in mounting terror as his hand began to explore her body. Afterwards all she could remember was the grip of his fingers on her throat and the harsh warmth of his lips on her mouth. There was heat, a blaze of power, the pressure of hard muscles taut in a hard, strong body, and then suddenly there was a dark dizziness before her eyes, a myriad points of flame seemed to burst in her head and she collapsed into merciful unconsciousness at his feet.

When Felicity came to she found that she was in bed, but the room was dark, the blinds shut to keep out the sun and she didn't know where she was. Her mouth and throat felt parched and her body ached intolerably. Softly she moaned and someone immediately came to her side and gave her a drink of water before bathing her face and hands and placing a cool cloth on her burning forehead. Who it was she was too ill to know, but whenever she waked, whenever she needed something, there was always someone there in the darkened room. At last she dropped into a deep feverless sleep, and when she woke many hours later she became fully conscious of her surroundings at last and realised that she was in her own room in Bruce's house.

Slowly she turned her head and saw Ellen sitting in a chair, placidly sewing. The movement must have caught the older woman's eye, for she immediately laid aside her embroidery frame and crossed to Felicity's side.

'So you're awake, at last? I was beginning to think I'd a Sleeping Beauty on my hands.' Her Scots burr was gentle as she felt Felicity's forehead and took her pulse. 'Aye,' she said with satisfaction, 'you're well over the worst. We'll have you up and about again in no time.'

156

Felicity was puzzled. 'Do you mean I've been ill?'

'Ill! Lord save us, child, you've had the 'flu! Not too badly, thank heaven, but enough to put you in bed for the last three days.'

'Three days!' Felicity could hardly believe it. 'Oh, Ellen, I'm sorry to have been such a nuisance. I seem to be making a habit of getting you to undress me and put me to bed.' She smiled weakly at the doctor's wife.

'Och, it wasn't me this time. Have you forgotten I was helping on Sancreed when the nurse there went down with the virus? I only got back to Trenaka yesterday.'

'Th-then who . . .'

'Why, lassie, who else but your husband? Bruce insisted on nursing you here himself and would still have been here if he hadn't had to fly to Barbados this morning on important business, although he refused to go until he knew for certain that you were over the worst.'

Felicity felt herself blushing all over, and it was nothing to do with her recent fever. 'How long will he be away?' she managed to ask.

'Only a few days, and by that time you should be back on your feet again.'

She was indeed better when he got back, although Mac had insisted that she had a few days of rest before returning to work. When Bruce walked into the house he dropped his suitcase in the hall and came straight to find her and ask how she was. Remembering what had happened on the night before her illness and his ministrations to her during it, she felt herself starting to blush and hastily turned away to hide her face.

Mistaking the reason for her action, he said sardonically, 'I see that my absence hasn't made any difference to you. Perhaps you were even glad to have me out of the way?'

'Just what is that supposed to mean?' Felicity turned to face him, the gratitude she had felt and meant to express ebbing swiftly away.

He gestured towards a bowl of yellow roses on the polished table. 'Who sent those? Another of your admirers?'

Clenching her fists, she retorted, 'Several of my *friends* sent me flowers.'

He looked down at her, a faint flicker of a sarcastic smile on his lips. 'You seem to be completely recovered?'

'Yes.'

'Good. I've booked a table at a night-club for eight o'clock. That should give you plenty of time to change, shouldn't it?'

'Yes.' Felicity looked at him uncertainly; they hadn't been out alone together since before their wedding. 'But why?'

'Have you forgotten the date? It's your birthday.'

'Oh!' She hadn't realised that Bruce even knew. She certainly hadn't broadcast the fact and, apart from a card from her mother sent on from the hospital, the day had been like any other. But now Bruce wanted to take her out. Her emotions were very mixed as she went to change into a simple, figure-hugging white dress and twisted her hair up into a chignon that made her look far more sophisticated than she was. She had lost weight during the recent weeks of work and tension, giving her figure the fashionably angular look.

Bruce gave her a glance of approval as he helped her out of the car at the night-club he had chosen, in an old plantation house where the atmosphere, dimly lit by candles, was warm and friendly. They ate, a gourmet's feast from a superb menu, and then danced and watched the cabaret. Felicity had been tense at first, ready to put up her defences against any overtures he might make, but Bruce talked casually of everyday things, told her one or two anecdotes that made her smile despite herself and held her very loosely when they danced. Gradually she relaxed with the help of several glasses of wine and lay back sleepily as they drove home.

'Want a nightcap?' Bruce asked as they went into the sitting-room.

'Mm, please.' Felicity went over to the stereo and put on a record.

Bruce came across with her drink and a small parcel. 'A birthday present. I thought I'd better give it to you here instead of the restaurant, just in case you decided to throw it back at me,' he said dryly, but there was a smile in his eyes.

Slowly Felicity reached up and took it from him. Inside was a gold coin set into a ring. 'Why, it's the coin we found in the wreck!'

'Yes, I had it cleaned and mounted while I was in Barbados.'

'Thank you, it's beautiful.' Felicity traced the outline of the ring with her finger tip, then, carefully not looking at him, she added, 'I wanted to thank you for looking after me when I was ill. I'm very grateful.'

'Don't be. It's my privilege to take care of you,' he said softly, then hesitated as if waiting for her to reply. When she didn't he said, 'Aren't you going to try on the ring?'

'Yes, of course.' Felicity took the gleaming golden circle from the box and slipped it on to the third finger of her right hand. 'It fits perfectly.'

'I had it made the same size as your wedding ring. Let's see how it looks.' Bruce took hold of her hand and drew her towards the lamp light. 'Yes, it suits the shape of your hand.' With his finger he gently began to stroke her wrist, then gradually moved up her arm.

Felicity felt herself begin to tremble, experienced the choking sensation in her throat and fast beating heart she always felt whenever he touched her. It happened suddenly but inevitably. In one quick movement he had taken her in his arms and crushed her tight against him. His mouth found hers in desperate, unconcealed longing and Felicity found herself returning his kiss with equal passion, caring for nothing but the bruising power of his lips and the warm masculine comfort of his arms. Her body ached with need and she clung even closer to him.

'Felicity, oh, my darling, I want you so much,' he said softly, hoarsely; but the spell was broken.

With a cry of repulsion, Felicity tore herself from his embrace, ashamed of her own emotions, loathing him for having awakened them in her. 'How dare you touch me!' She wiped her mouth with the back of her hand. 'Do you think I want your horrible kisses? I can't stand it when you touch me. I hate you! I hate you!'

'Hate me? Because I want to be the same as every other man and love my wife?'

'No, because you're a liar and a murderer and ...' She stopped aghast. In her fury because he had made her forget for a moment that he was her enemy, had made her treacherous body respond to his kisses, she had gone too far. Quickly she turned to run out of the room. The brass door handle was cool against her palm, she tried to turn it, but Bruce put his hand over hers and stopped her.

'Oh, no, you don't. You've got some explaining to do.'

Felicity backed away from him until brought up short by the wall. She placed both hands against it and stood perfectly still, too frightened to move.

'Just what did you mean by that last remark?'

'N-nothing.'

'Don't lie to me! You let something slip, and I'm going to find out what it is.' His hand was at her throat, lifting her chin, making her look at him. 'Are you going to tell me, or do I have to force it out of you? I can, you know,' he said unpleasantly.

Felicity stared up at him, seeing the determined set of his jaw and the cold ruthlessness in his eyes. It had to be the truth now, she realised. There could be no more lies, no more pretence. It was over and she had lost. Better not to even think what he might do to her when he knew the truth. She was the loser and she must take whatever retribution he cared to inflict on her. But she wouldn't grovel in front of him; he might have defeated her, but she had fought on till the end! Looking him straight in the eyes, she said clearly, 'All right, you shall have the truth. My real name isn't Lambert, it's Callison. And you murdered my brother Peter!'

He took in a sharp breath as if he had been hit, then said, with utter weariness, 'Oh, my God!'

'I took the post on Trenaka knowing that you were here and I came with the express intention of ruining you in any way I could. At first I couldn't think of a way, but then you insisted on marrying me and the solution was obvious.'

Slowly, as if with a tremendous effort, he said, his voice rasping hoarsely in his throat, 'And when we were at Jabalya Key, on our wedding night? You had already planned to run away and leave me behind?'

She nodded, unable to speak.

'And the story you told me afterwards on the boat? It was all a lie? A lie to cover up because you couldn't get away, wasn't it?'

Felicity tried to look away, unable to bear the deep, dark pain in his eyes, unable to bear the turmoil of fear inside herself; but he dragged her head up again and locked his hands on either side of her face. 'Answer me, Felicity. Answer me!'

'Yes.' It was such a small word, but it meant so much.

'You bitch! You beautiful, cheating bitch!' With infinite slowness he let go of her, a look of unconcealed pain and fury on his face. Then he hit her, just once, hard across the face. She staggered but didn't fall, almost welcoming the pain that gave her a chance to close her eyes to the agony that she had caused. She knew that she ought to be glad; ought to be revelling in hurting him, but she found no pleasure in what she had done.

When she opened her eyes at last Bruce was standing with his back to her, his shoulders hunched, his hands gripping the back of a chair until his knuckles showed white. Felicity could only guess at the effort it must have cost him to turn to face her, his face white and set, but fully in control of his emotions. He looked at her contemptuously, his

161

every word a knife thrust. 'I apologise. I shouldn't have done that. It's never worth losing one's temper over liars and cheats.'

Deliberately he turned the chair round and sat facing her, leaning back in insolent ease, his legs crossed; only his hands gripping the armrests betraying his inner feelings.

His voice was hard, bitter, as he said, 'I certainly played into your hands, didn't I? The poor besotted fool who fell in love with the girl who was willing to lie, cheat, break the most sacred promises, do anything, in order to destroy him. No wonder I caused such a reaction in you. How you must have laughed when I told you I loved you!'

'No, I didn't laugh.' Felicity began to tremble uncontrollably. 'I was glad that it would soon be over. Because I hated you! I've hated you all through the years of grief and sadness that you caused my mother! I promised her that I would make you pay for what you did, promised to be revenged. My brother's dead and you're alive and prosperous. You were doing well, making a name for yourself. The only name my brother has is on his tombstone!' She broke off, unable to go on, her breath coming in great sobs, her heart beating wildly.

Bruce had risen to his feet now and came towards her. She flinched away from him, pressing herself against the wall. 'Don't touch me! I hate it when you touch me!'

A muscle tightened in his jaw, but he had himself under iron control. Urgently he said, 'You've got to listen to me. You were only about fifteen when your brother was killed. You couldn't possibly have known the true facts. I swear to you that I didn't kill your brother!'

'Oh, not with your own hands, perhaps,' she said scornfully. 'But it was you who drove him away in such a terrible state that he crashed his car and was burnt to death!'

'He came to my mother's house in an attempt to make my young sister run away with him. He'd been seeing Camilla in secret because he knew we wouldn't approve. But I found out and convinced her that he wanted her only because my father had left her a large sum of money which she would inherit when she married. She refused to go with him and your brother turned nasty and tried to take her by force. Luckily I heard her cries for help and gave him the thrashing he deserved. It was due entirely to his own weakness of character that he then went out and got drunk, and afterwards crashed that Jaguar that he was incapable of controlling properly even when he was sober.'

'How dare you! How dare you say such horrible things about Peter! He was in love with your sister and she with him. He came home that night and told us that you'd forced them apart, knocked him down and then dragged Camilla back into the house. He was absolutely broken-hearted! He had never loved anyone but your sister and he was in despair that she would be sent away. He said that he was going back to offer to wait, to plead with you not to send her away ...' Felicity was crying now, tears that coursed unheeded down her cheeks.

'Felicity, none of that was true! Your brother was a scoundrel. He'd already got more than one local girl pregnant and had himself been in trouble with the police. He never held a job for more than a couple of months, and he twisted your poor mother round his little finger, making her give him money for fast cars, clothes, anything he wanted. And what he wanted, he took. It's the truth, Felicity! I went into his background when I first found out he was seeing my sister. Do you think that I would let her even contemplate marriage to such a man? He would have gone through her money and left her destitute within six months!'

Felicity put her hands over her ears, but she couldn't shut out his stinging accusations. Her face was white with anger, her eyes lost in tears. 'That isn't true! None of it! Peter was a wonderful person. You're only saying that to try to justify what you did. You're lying, I tell you! You're lying!'

Bruce's voice was controlled, heavy. 'No, Felicity. I've

163

never lied to you. That is your family's prerogative.'

She looked at him, her eyes dark and staring. Even after all that she had done to him he would not admit his guilt. She had never felt so completely and utterly defeated, and knew that she could stand no more. Numbly, she managed to push herself away from the wall and went blindly from the room.

CHAPTER NINE

DURING the night there was another great storm that whipped the branches of the trees and drowned the noises of the small garden creatures. Felicity welcomed the storm, throwing open the window to let the wind and the rain blow in on her as she sat on the window sill. Hours ago she had cried herself out and then had deliberately set about packing her belongings. There wasn't a lot, really, just her clothes and a few personal possessions, like the coral candlesticks that David had sent to her, and the tablecloth that Ellen had embroidered with her own hands. Those she couldn't bear to leave behind.

As her boss, Mac was certainly due for some explanation, but in her letter to him Felicity merely said that she had received an urgent summons from England, and left it at that. Bruce could add further explanations or not, as he wished.

So now she had nothing to do but sit and watch the storm and wait. The morning plane bringing the day trippers from Jamaica would arrive at ten-thirty; all she had to do was to order a car to take her to the airport. From here she could see the curve of the bay, the sea blown into flurrying white horses by the storm, but as the night passed the storm passed with it, and soon the first light of dawn began to appear in the sky. The dark purple of night fell away to let in the pale colours from above and the surging light of the sun from below. The sun slipped clear of the sea in perfect red roundness and began its steady climb, wiping the sky clear of strong colours and washing it in a delicate blue. Soon the red would fade to white and bring the intense heat of the day.

Bruce always left the house for his office at seven-thirty. Felicity waited until eight o'clock and then walked downstairs to the study to telephone for a taxi, the letter to Mac and her smaller suitcase in her hands. But as she entered the study Bruce swivelled his chair round to face her, his eyes cold, the fingers of each hand together in a pyramid. 'Going somewhere?'

For a moment she stared at him stupidly. 'I thought you'd gone to the office.'

'It's Saturday.'

'Oh! Is it?' She put up a hand to push her hair off her forehead, feeling completely unable to cope with this new situation.

'I asked you if you were going somewhere?'

'To—to England.'

'And leaving me a letter of farewell? How very thoughtful of you!' His look and tone were full of contempt.

She flinched, but said, 'No, it's for Mac.'

'Give it to me.'

'I told you, it's for Mac.'

'And I said, give it to me! I want to see what lies you've told this time.'

Two bright spots of colour appeared high on her cheekbones, but obediently she gave him the letter and waited for him to open it. Bruce merely glanced at the inscription and then tore it into four.

'But—but why?'

'Because you're not going anywhere! Do you think I don't see what you're trying to do? By running away now you would create almost as much scandal as you tried to make before. The minute you got back to England you would be writing to Ellen to tell her another pack of foul lies! And perhaps even to the Steventons and everyone else here to make absolutely certain you spread the dirt properly.'

166

Felicity stared at him askance. 'But I wouldn't. I give you my word I wouldn't.'

'Your word!' He laughed derisively.

'Can't you understand?' Felicity said desperately. 'It's over! You've won; I've lost. We can both be free of one another. You can have the marriage annulled. I'll sign any papers, any—confession—you like. Agree to anything you want. But I have to get away from here, don't you see that?'

'I see that you want to get away, but why should I let you go so easily? I've put up with a great deal at your hands, and I don't see why you should be let off so lightly.'

'Please let me go, Bruce. I've told you I'll agree to anything you want,' she pleaded.

He rose from his chair and looked at her intently, his eyes dropping down over her tall, slender body with insolent appraisal. 'Anything—I want?'

Colouring with mortification under his gaze, Felicity said painfully, 'No, not anything.'

'I thought not,' he said with cool disdain, and Felicity realised that he had deliberately set out to trap her, like a cat playing with a mouse. 'So you'll just have to stay here where I can keep an eye on you.'

'But we can't go on like—like this, indefinitely.'

'I have no intention of doing so. Your term of contract as assistant to Mac is for three years. At the end of that period, if you've behaved yourself, I'll allow you to return to England.'

Felicity stared at him aghast. 'Three years!'

'Three years.' His eyes narrowed and he reached out to touch her hair. 'Unless, of course, you would prefer to pay the alternative price, now?'

Swirling her hair away from him, Felicity said balefully, 'A lifetime would be better than that!' Then she turned and walked away from him, her chin tilted defiantly, her heart like lead.

The large, liquid dark eyes of the little native girl looked up at Felicity trustingly as, with gentle fingers, she treated the large burn on the child's leg. It must have been extremely painful, but the girl hardly whimpered as the dressings were applied. Fortunately the parents lived quite near, so Felicity was able to arrange for them to bring the child in regularly for treatment instead of having to keep her in. The mother thanked her shyly before carrying the girl away. Watching them walk out of the surgery, Felicity swallowed a harsh lump in her throat. What was it—self-pity? she wondered. Well, she had brought it on herself, so she would just have to learn to live with it. She sighed and rang for the next patient. All this would wear off in time, of course, but not the love she had for her job. Never that. She remembered that Bruce had once said that work, although a great panacea, wasn't enough. For her it would have to be enough.

As she popped a sweet into the mouth of her last small patient, Felicity felt someone watching her and looked up to see Geoff eyeing her tolerantly.

'No wonder they all want to come to see you. Don't you know it's strictly unethical to bribe the patients?'

'A poor girl has to do something,' she retorted, wrinkling up her nose at him.

Geoff regarded her thoughtfully, his professional eye noting how thin she had become and the dark, pinched look on her face. 'You don't look exactly one hundred per cent fit yourself. You sure you should have come back to work so soon?'

'Quite sure,' she said shortly.

'All right, don't snap my head off. You're the doctor.'

'I'm sorry, Geoff.' Felicity looked at him contritely. 'Pax?'

'Pax,' he grinned amiably. 'Well, I'm off. I promised to play tennis at the Residency, although I wonder I bother. Now that you've given yourself over to wedded bliss the only eligible girl is Diane, and all she did the last time was to get in a huddle with David. And I bet you won't guess in a million years what they were talking about?'

168

With a flash of intuition, Felicity replied, 'I bet I can. Market gardens.'

Geoff shook his head wonderingly. 'How did *you* know? No one ever tells me anything,' he grumbled, and went off to his bungalow to change.

As slowly as she could, Felicity took off her working clothes and changed her shoes, taking her time over washing her hands and combing her hair so that there would be less time to spend at Bruce's house. She could never think of it as home. Home is where you're happy; she had never had one minute of happiness since her fatal marriage. Edwina, too, was preparing to leave and wished her a cheerful goodbye as she passed the desk. For some unaccountable reason she thought of Diane and David having deep discussions about market gardens, and she was still smiling about it when she came out of the hospital.

'How pleasant to see you smile.' Bruce was leaning against the car, his arms folded, as he waited for her. His voice was sarcastic and Felicity's features immediately set into the fixed expressionless mask that she had habitually come to assume whenever she was with him during the two weeks since his return from Barbados. 'I see it wasn't a smile of welcome for me,' he added dryly.

'It isn't necessary for you to meet me. I have a car.'

'It would hardly be very lover-like if I drove right by without picking you up, would it?' he said as he opened the door for her.

Drawing into the corner of the seat, Felicity didn't answer him. Dully she wondered how on earth she could go on. She had known it would be bad, but never as bad as this. He had made the rules and he forced her to obey them. It was all right when she was working, but then there were the long evenings to be got through; the coldly polite mealtimes and the never-ending weekends. Mostly she tried not to think, not to feel, but always there was a dull ache of misery deep inside her.

Silently they sat down to the dinner that Jemima had

cooked for them and afterwards Felicity rose, intending to go to her room. He let her get as far as the door, then said her name savagely. Quivering, she hesitated, then stopped.

'Sit down! I haven't said you can go yet.'

'No! You can't treat me like this. It's inhuman!'

'Really? And what would you call your treatment of me? You haven't begun to learn the half of it yet. I've only just started to teach you what it's like to go through hell! Now, sit down again.'

Slowly, reluctantly, she obeyed him.

'Hey, Felicity! Can you spare a few minutes?'

Turning in surprise, Felicity saw Geoff running along the path behind her. 'Where are you off to?' he asked, panting.

'You are out of condition. I thought I'd walk into Trenaka to do some shopping.'

'Don't you know only mad dogs and Englishmen go out in the midday sun?'

'Well, I feel rather like a mad dog today.'

He looked at her narrowly. 'Anything wrong, old girl? It hasn't been exactly roses all the way, has it?'

Smiling wanly, Felicity said, 'It's something I have to work out for myself, Geoff.'

He nodded. 'Point taken. But I wanted to talk to you. I wanted to ask you to do something for me, something that you may not want to do and also that Bruce might not approve of. But there's no one else I can ask, and it's something that means more to me than anything has ever done before.'

Coming to a standstill, Felicity looked at him intently. She had never known Geoff like this before. All his old cynicism was gone and he was deadly serious. 'You'd better tell me what it is,' she said.

'There's a café just along the street. We can talk there.'

Sitting in the shade of a gaily striped awning, Geoff ordered cold drinks and waited until they had been served.

170

To Felicity's surprise he seemed somewhat embarrassed, fiddling about with his glass before clearing his throat and running a finger round his collar. 'Well—er—you see, it's like this . . .'

Looking at him with some amusement, Felicity said encouragingly, 'Well, come on, it can't be that bad.'

He looked at her seriously. 'Yes, Felicity, it is. You see I've fallen head over heels in love and—well, it's a bit awkward.'

Felicity went cold. 'What do you want of me?'

'I want you to help us to get away from Trenaka until the fuss dies down.'

Staring at him in horror, Felicity said, 'You mean you intend to return?'

'Yes, just as soon as I'm sure of our welcome.'

'Welcome! You must be mad. And if you think I'm going to help you do anything so sordid, then you're wrong. Completely wrong!'

Geoff's mouth hardened into a bitter line. 'I should have known better than to ask you. For a while I thought you would be on my side, but anyone who marries just for position is bound to be afraid of anything that might hurt her social ambitions!'

'Geoff, if you don't shut up, I'll hit you! And if you think I'm going to help you to steal another man's wife, you're crazy!' she said heatedly.

It was Geoff's turn to stare. 'Another man's . . .? What are you talking about?'

'I'm not going to help you run off with Gillian, Geoff, and that's final!'

'Gillian? I haven't seen her for weeks. Except that time she trod on the sea-urchin and you brought her to the hospital. We had a blazing row that day because I'd been trying to avoid her. As a matter of fact, I wouldn't put it past her to have seen the sea-urchin and trodden on it deliberately just to make an excuse to see me. Anyway, as I said, we had a hell of a row because she'd become too possessive and de-

171

manding. Wanting me to have an affair and take her away from Trenaka. Gillian just got too serious, and besides ... well, I'd already fallen for somebody else.'

'The person you want to run away with instead?'

'I don't want to run away with her. Or, at least, I want to marry her first, then to go away for a bit and come back after everyone's got over the first shock.'

'How are the mighty fallen!' Felicity couldn't help teasing him a little. 'And you the confirmed bachelor who was only going to "love 'em and leave 'em". You'd better tell me who this paragon is, who has finally brought you to your knees.'

'It's ...' He looked at her uncertainly, as if afraid of what she might say. 'It's Edwina!'

Felicity managed to keep the surprise from her face. She was pretty good at not showing her feelings nowadays; it comes in handy, she thought detachedly. She smiled at Geoff. 'Congratulations. I couldn't be more pleased. She's a very fine person.'

He flushed, a look of pride in his eyes. 'She is, isn't she? And she's had a really bad deal out of life so far; I want to make up to her for that. But it isn't going to be easy. She isn't accepted in the Residency circle, and you know what Lady Steventon's like.'

'Do I!' Felicity said with feeling, remembering Lady Steventon's attempt to squash her before she got engaged to Bruce. The more gentle and docile Edwina would never be able to stand up to such an interview and would get terribly hurt in the process, probably being convinced that she was ruining Geoff's life by marrying him. 'I'll help all I can, of course. What do you plan to do?'

'Next week there's a carnival on the island to celebrate some anniversary or other. There are bound to be the usual bands and parades. Well, I thought that while all that was going on we could slip away and catch a plane to Jamaica. I've applied for a special licence and it will be waiting for us at the Register Office in Kingston. Then I'll arrange for a notice of the wedding to be put in the local rag so that when we come back it will already be an accepted thing.'

'But where do I come in? Do you want me to help Edwina choose a wedding dress, or something?'

'Nothing so simple. I want you to come to Jamaica with us to be a witness at the wedding.'

'Go to Jamaica? But I can't! Bruce would never . . .' She broke off and stared at Geoff in consternation.

'I know it's a lot to ask, but I've had a hell of a job persuading Edwina to marry me. She's afraid that all the Service people will ostracise us. She's only worried for me, not for herself, Felicity. She said she couldn't bear it if all my friends dropped me. That's why there's got to be someone from the crowd to back us up, to stand our friend. Edwina has a cousin in Jamaica who will act as the other witness, but she didn't want it to be all one-sided, as if I was giving up everything for her.'

Privately Felicity wondered just how much Geoff would have to give up, but she said at once, 'Of course I'll come to Jamaica. I'm very honoured that you should ask me. But, Geoff, what about getting time off?'

'I've got two weeks' leave due to me and Mac's bound to let you have the day off as it's your first big carnival. The only problem is that Bruce might want to take you. Do you think he will?'

She said steadily, 'I shouldn't think so. He's very busy at the moment. But, Geoff, I'll be awfully late getting back from Jamaica. The night plane that takes the day trippers back doesn't get here until nearly midnight.'

'No problem. I've hired a private plane.'

Felicity looked at him. 'You knew all along I'd say yes, didn't you?'

He grinned. 'Well, I knew you wouldn't be able to resist watching me get my ball and chain attached.'

'You're incorrigible!' Then suddenly serious, she said slowly, 'Geoff, I—er—I think it would be better if we didn't say anything about this to Bruce. I'll be back before he has a chance to miss me and he ... Well, he might not understand.'

Geoff covered her small hand with his big brown one. 'I couldn't agree more, old girl,' he said fervently.

When she got back to the hospital Felicity found a letter from England waiting for her. As her mother had always addressed her letters care of the hospital it came as no surprise. With reluctant fingers Felicity opened the envelope, already guessing the contents. She was not mistaken; Mrs Lambert blamed her for not taking any action against Bruce, berated her for looking to her own amusements when she should have been bringing about Bruce's downfall. The words were harsh, vitriolic. Every other line contained Peter's name 'Peter will never lie easy in his grave until you have avenged him! Don't you want him to lie at peace? It doesn't matter what you have to do. It doesn't matter if your name comes into it. God will curse you if you don't act at once. Peter will curse you ...'

It was worse than it had ever been before. The writing was scrawled, uneven; in some places she could hardly read it. The words were those of a sick, neurotic woman. Hastily Felicity folded the letter and stuffed it into her pocket as she heard Mac's footsteps approaching, then put on her overall and went to do her ward round. But later, when she was checking through some records, her mind wandered back to the letter and she wondered how on earth she was to answer. It was impossible to keep her travesty of a marriage from her mother for ever, but how to tell her that she was completely within the power of her enemy? Mrs Lambert was not physically strong, years of grief and hate had undermined her strength. But she would have to know, somehow Felicity would have to find the words to tell her.

In less than a week, however, on the eve of the carnival and before Felicity had done more than attempt to compose an answer in her mind, she received a cablegram informing her of her mother's death. It had been sent by the firm of solicitors handling Mrs Lambert's estate and was brief and to the point. 'Regret advise death Mrs Elizabeth Lambert due severe stroke. Funeral Friday'. At first there was no reaction. She was clear-headed and calm, looking at the cablegram without it touching her emotions. The funeral was on Friday; but that was tomorrow! There must have been a delay in reaching her, and on looking at the address she saw that it had originally been sent to the wrong group of islands before being forwarded to Trenaka, causing several days' delay. If she chartered a plane to Jamaica she might be able to catch a scheduled flight if there was an empty seat, which seemed unlikely in the height of the season. Even if she did get to England by tomorrow there was still the time difference, and she would also have to travel down to Bournemouth where her mother had been living.

Picking up the telephone, she asked for the number of the local charter plane service, but then the other implications began to seep into her mind. Geoff's wedding! She had promised faithfully to go to the ceremony; but surely he wouldn't hold her to it in the light of her news? But Geoff, like everyone else, except Bruce, thought that she was an orphan, brought up by a distant aunt. Then there was Bruce himself—would he let her go? He would be more likely to think that she had arranged to have the cable sent to her by a friend in England; that it was just a ruse so that she could get away from him and have a legitimate excuse in the eyes of her friends on Trenaka to go back to England. To go and never come back!

A voice crackled on the other end of the line.

'It—it doesn't matter. I made a mistake.' Slowly she put down the receiver and looked again at the cable. There was a third factor to be taken into consideration, one that she had not allowed herself to even remotely think about before. But this news had made her suddenly stop and let her feelings take over. Closing her eyes, she let the numbing pain in her heart spread through her whole being. She knew that

175

she couldn't go on pretending, fighting, running away any more. She didn't want to go back to England. She didn't want to leave Trenaka. Because she was in love with Bruce; in love with a man who despised her and wanted only to hurt and humiliate her!

Felicity realised that she had known in her heart ever since the night of her birthday when he had kissed her so passionately and she had responded with equal intensity. He had said that he would show her what it was like to go through hell, and only now was she beginning to realise the enormity of what she had done to him. She had set out to destroy another human being in the cruellest way possible; by destroying his faith in the woman he loved. For he had loved her once, before she had taken his love and crushed it into a nothingness.

For a long time she sat alone, accepting this love that had come too late, and with the acknowledgement came some little inner peace. It would be terribly hard, but from somewhere she would find the courage to bear it. And she would not attempt to go to England, where she would probably have been too late anyway. Instead she would go to the wedding and try to do a little good for all the harm she had caused.

Later that night, just as the sun was about to set, she went down through the garden, gathering flowers as she walked. Bruce had come home early and for once seemed strangely quiet as if waiting for something, but at least he hadn't tried to stop her when she left the house. The tide was ebbing as she reached the shore. She slipped off her shoes and walked across the beach to where some rocks jutted out into the sea. Felicity climbed out to the furthest rock, still carrying her armful of flowers. Silhouetted against the sky, she looked across the sea at the brilliant redness of the setting sun. In a moment, she knew, it would be gone.

'I'm sorry, Mother,' Felicity whispered, and one by one tossed the flowers into the sea and watched them drift away on the tide. When the last one had disappeared she turned away and walked slowly back to the house.

A few minutes later Bruce moved away from the tree he had been leaning against and followed her, a thoughtful look in his eyes.

CHAPTER TEN

FROM every lamp-post there hung baskets of cascading flowers and buntings; the air was alive with the noise of a dozen steel bands, all playing different calypsos or revivalist songs as they danced, rather than marched their way through the streets of Trenaka town. Each band outvied the others in the brilliance of dress, their colourful costumes scintillating with thousands of sequins which reflected the bright, hot sunshine. Energetic policemen in their short-sleeved shirts and white pith helmets blew whistles and waved their arms frantically in a vain attempt to try and control the bands, the crowds of onlookers, and the many cars and bicycles that still insisted on using the roadways, their honking horns and ringing bells adding to the general noise and tumult.

Edwina lived in a small rooming-house down one of the quieter side streets, but the entrance to this was blocked temporarily by a group of limbo-dancers, one of whom was straining to get under the pole at only an incredible eighteen inches from the ground, and being urged on by shouts of excited encouragement from the crowd who had gathered round to watch. Geoff stopped the car and waited in good-humoured impatience, giving Felicity a grin. 'It's no use trying to hurry them out of the way. Let's hope they don't try to lower the pole again.'

Another steel band was coming along behind them, and as Felicity tapped her foot to the tune the tense build-up to the day was forgotten. The dancers moved on and the crowd opened to let them through.

Edwina looked lovely in a cream-coloured lace dress, and

178

she smiled rather shyly as Felicity insisted that she sit in the front seat with Geoff on the short ride to the airport. The Piper Cherokee that Geoff had hired was ready and waiting for them outside a hangar some distance away from the main buildings. The pilot checked to see that their passports were in order, looking up in some surprise when he saw Felicity's. He said nothing, however, and merely helped them aboard before going into the cockpit. Indistinctly they heard him talking over the radio to the control tower, and then the small plane taxied to the runway and was soon smoothly, efficiently, airborne.

Geoff grinned and gave a mock sigh of relief. 'Well, if anyone does miss us, at least they won't know which one of you I'm running away with!' he joked.

'They'll probably think it's both of us!' Edwina returned flippantly.

Felicity smiled; Edwina obviously knew just how to handle this man she had captured.

'I've arranged for a celebration meal after the wedding at a first-class restaurant in Kingston. But don't worry, Felicity, we'll get you back to the airport in plenty of time to get back to Trenaka.'

Compared to Trenaka town, Kingston was a full-sized city, and in normal circumstances Felicity would have enjoyed exploring like all the other tourists who thronged the busy streets, but Geoff had a hired car waiting for them that whisked them to the Register Office where the ceremony was to take place. Edwina's cousin and his family were already there, and Felicity liked them on sight. The cousin was a lawyer, a man of some standing in Jamaica, and he and his wife and two teenage children were well dressed and quietly spoken.

Shafts of sunlight shone down through the windows in the room where the wedding was performed and Edwina and Geoff stood very close as they took their vows. It reminded Felicity so poignantly of her own wedding just a few short weeks ago. But she had made hers a mockery.

179

She could have had love and happiness, but she had been so filled with hate and the need for revenge that she had refused to recognise the feelings that Bruce aroused in her for what they were, using them instead to sharpen her antagonism towards him.

And this morning had come the bitter proof that she had been completely unjustified in her actions. Bruce had driven her to the hospital as usual, she had scarcely looked at him, but all the same was forcefully conscious of his nearness. Their journey had been a silent one, but as he opened the door for her to alight, he hesitated and seemed about to say something, but then he made a dismissive gesture, merely saying, 'I'll pick you up this evening. Don't go into the town today, it can be pretty hectic during carnival.' Felicity had said nothing in reply, not daring to think of his reactions if he ever found out what she intended to do.

Mac looked up in surprise as she walked into the office. 'I thought you were off to the carnival, lassie?'

'I just looked in to make sure everything was okay.'

'Well now, I think I may just be able to manage on my own for one day,' he teased her. 'But it's just as well you looked in. This airmail letter arrived for you this morning.'

Glancing at her watch, Felicity saw that she still had ten minutes before she was due to meet Geoff, so she poured herself a cup of coffee from Mac's ever-filled percolator and took the letter out into the garden. Tearing open the envelope she found a letter inside from her mother's cousin, Elspeth, who still lived in Alnswick. After the usual expressions of condolence on her loss, Felicity was devastated to read: 'I do hope you're happy in Trenaka, my dear, and not taking any notice of those silly ideas for revenge that your poor mother was always going on about. I had no idea when I told her, two years ago, that Bruce Gresham had gone there to start a tour of duty, that she would be on the lookout for a job for you on the island. I almost wished I hadn't told her, but she was so insistent that I always let her know the latest news about him. But then

I'm afraid she hasn't really been the same since your poor brother was killed. She was completely overcome with grief, saying all sorts of silly things, when everyone knows that Peter was always getting drunk and was bound to crash that car of his one day.

'I couldn't say it to your mother, of course, because she just wouldn't listen, but in a way it was a blessed relief that he died when he did. What with having to pay off that man he injured in a brawl, and keeping up the payments on the affiliation orders, as well as paying his court fines and setting him up with the car when he came out of Borstal— well, it's a wonder your poor mother wasn't even more unbalanced than she was!'

The letter went on about other things, but Felicity hardly took them in. So her mother had lied to her when she had said that she only found out about Bruce being in Trenaka *after* Felicity had got the job there. All the time she had intended that Felicity should bring about his ruin, with no thought for her daughter's feelings. But surely no normal person would ... But with sinking heart she realised that her mother hadn't been completely normal since Peter's death; that the accident had twisted and embittered her mind until she wasn't a rational person any more. And almost she had done the same to Felicity. Almost, but not quite, although it had cost her the love of the man she now wanted more than anything else in the world. But he had loved her once; she still had that knowledge to treasure. And she still had nearly three years in which to atone for what she had done. Perhaps by the time it came for them to part he would—not love her, or even like her, that was quite impossible now—but perhaps he wouldn't hate her quite so much.

Geoff had hailed her, but she had asked him to wait for a moment, and then gone into the office to take her photograph of Peter from the drawer where she had locked it away just before her marriage. Then she ran into the room near the surgery where all the soiled bandages and swabs

181

were incinerated. Without hesitation she thrust the photograph into its glowing interior and shut down the lid to let the past burn away.

The wedding breakfast was a happy one, everyone feeling more relaxed now that the ceremony was over, but Felicity was beginning to feel rather anxious about the time. The eldest teenager had turned out to be a keen photographer and had insisted on taking several shots, with the result that they had been late arriving at the restaurant and found that their table had been taken by someone else and they had to wait for another to be vacated. Waiting had been pleasant enough in the well-appointed bar, but the meal, too, had been protracted and the party showed no signs of breaking up.

Catching at his sleeve, Felicity said in an urgent whisper, 'Geoff, I have to get back to the airport. It's nearly three o'clock.'

Geoff smote his head, 'Sorry, Felicity, I clean forgot the time. I'll get a taxi and take you there.'

'Find me a taxi, yes, but don't bother to take me yourself. I can manage perfectly well alone.'

Although he protested, Geoff didn't really want to leave his bride and he was eventually persuaded to see her off after telling her exactly where to find the pilot of the Cherokee.

'Thanks for everything, Felicity. You're one in a million. If I wasn't a married man I'd probably kiss you.'

Felicity laughed. 'Good luck, Geoff. Be happy!' She blew him a kiss and then the taxi was hurrying to the airport.

The concourse was crowded with people and presented the usual scene of utter confusion that characterised every airport anywhere in the world. Looking at the piece of paper on which Geoff had hastily scribbled the directions, Felicity tried to push her way through to the gateway she wanted, but found herself mixed up with a bevy of home-going Americans in their luridly patterned shirts and straw hats who were heading for another departure gate.

Suddenly she found herself grabbed by the arm and yanked forcibly out of the crowd. Turning her startled head, she found herself staring into a pair of blazing grey eyes.

'Oh, no!' she breathed in dismay.

'Oh, yes!' His voice was vicious. 'Another of your pleasant little tricks, wasn't it, to enlist Geoff's help to get you to Jamaica? What did you promise the poor devil as a reward?'

Felicity coloured painfully at his words and their implication. She tried to speak, but Bruce cut her short. 'And where is he now? Did you dump him when he'd served his purpose?'

Still holding her arm, he led her, far from gently, to a gateway where they were let through by the official, with a smart salute for Bruce and not even a request to see their passports. On the tarmac waited a small, single-engined plane, and Bruce reached up and opened the door for her to climb in.

'But I already have ...'

'Get in!' he ordered, his eyes dangerous.

Felicity got in. She only hoped the pilot of the Cherokee wouldn't hang around too long for her before returning to Trenaka. Bruce climbed into the pilot's seat beside her and to Felicity's amazement put on the headset and proceeded to ask the control tower for clearance. He handled the little plane easily and well so that Felicity had no fear as she sat beside him—not of his abilities as a pilot, anyway. When they were clear of the busy airlanes above Jamaica and on a course for Trenaka, he relaxed a little and turned off the headset.

'I didn't know you could fly.'

'There's a lot you don't know about me.'

Rebuked, Felicity sat silent for a while, then roused herself to ask, 'How did you find me?'

'All charter flights have to give details of their passengers to the authorities before take-off. The officer on duty happened to remark to me that he was surprised you should be leaving on a carnival day.'

Felicity sighed. She should have known it was inevitable that he would find out.

As if guessing her thoughts, he said, 'Just remember that I know everything that goes on in Trenaka, Felicity. Whatever trick you pull, whichever way you run, I shall always find you and drag you back. I'm not letting you go until I'm good and ready to kick you out!'

For a few minutes she toyed with the idea of telling him about the wedding and the plane still waiting back in Jamaica, but she dismissed the thought almost immediately. Even if he believed her he would only use the knowledge to increase his hold over her. She realised that by now he must have given up all thoughts of happiness. It hurt unbearably.

At last they touched down in Trenaka and Bruce taxied the plane towards a hangar. He talked to the mechanic there for a short time and then walked her across to where the car was waiting in the shade of a hut. Felicity lay back in the seat and closed her eyes, feeling utterly weary. On the streets the carnival was still in full swing and had been joined by bands from neighbouring islands together with hordes of visiting tourists. Bruce obviously knew the geography of the town intimately, for he threaded his way through the back streets, only having to touch the main road once or twice, the crowd parting cheerfully for him as soon as they saw the Government flag on the bonnet and recognised the driver.

Arriving at the house, Felicity made to go to her room, but Bruce put an arm out to stop her. 'I want a few words with you,' he said grimly.

Felicity turned to him, too weary and numb to feel afraid any more. 'You can say what you want, call me what names you like, but first I'm hot and sticky and I'm going to have a swim before I change.'

He looked at her intently, noting the dark shadows round

her eyes, the white, set look on her face, then wordlessly lowered his arm to let her pass.

The sea was calm and cool, a balm to her tired mind and body. She floated on her back for some time and then climbed up to the rocks where she could sit and let her mind go blank. Possibly she dozed, for the next thing she knew Bruce was calling her name harshly from where he stood below her. The tide had started to come in and he was almost up to his chest in the sea. 'You've been out here long enough. Get down and come back to the house.'

Perhaps it was his tone, perhaps it was the scorn in his eyes that brought back a flash of her old spirit. 'What's the matter? Frightened I might drown myself and escape from you that way?'

'I wouldn't put it past you even to do that, you little coward.' He reached out to grab her, but Felicity moved nimbly out of the way.

'Afraid I might cheat you out of the satisfaction you'd get from years of punishing me?' she taunted him.

With a sharp expletive, Bruce waded between two rocks and catching her wrist, pulled her bodily into the water. Spluttering, she came to the surface, the tide reaching her shoulders. Her burst of rebellion suitably dampened, she turned to precede him to the beach, but heard a sudden exclamation behind her.

'My foot's caught in something.' Taking a deep breath, Bruce ducked down into the sea, but came up a few moments later, gasping and shaking the water from his eyes, a grim look on his face. 'It's a giant clam. It's closed itself on my foot and I can't prise it open.' He looked at her steadily. 'You'll have to help me, Felicity.'

For a moment fear held her frozen as it had when she couldn't find him at Jabalya Key. Why, oh, why hadn't she realised then that it was love she felt? She became aware that he was watching her, a dark, lost look in his eyes. 'What do you want me to do?'

There was a new note in his voice as he said, 'You pull one side, I'll pull the other.'

They dived simultaneously and pulled with all their strength, but it was no use; the clam was shut tight and wouldn't be budged.

'You'll have to find some sort of a lever,' Bruce gasped as they came up for air.

Finding a piece of tree branch on the beach, Felicity had to swim part of the way back, for the tide was now well in and almost up to Bruce's shoulders. 'Good girl,' he said, taking it from her.

'Shall I get the air-tanks?'

'No good, they're on the boat down at the harbour.' He got the branch inside the shell and exerted all his pressure while Felicity pulled, but there was a sharp crack and the branch broke in two.

Felicity didn't stop to look at Bruce as she swam as fast as she could for the shore. It seemed an age until she reached the house and ran round to the garage, the pain, as she trod on some sharp stones with her bare feet, unheeded. Fortunately the boot of the car was unlocked; her frantic fingers quickly found what she sought, but her hands were wet and the tyre lever slipped and fell clanging to the ground. With a sob she went down on her knees to pick it up and then ran as she had never known she could back to the beach.

The sea was right up to Bruce's chin now, but there was a curious light in his eyes as she swam up to him. 'Steady now, don't drop it.'

He took the lever and plunged down, but had to come up again shortly for air; he couldn't get a deep enough breath with the waves lapping over him. But Felicity could. Taking the lever from him, she dived again and got a good purchase. Using every last ounce of her strength she pressed on the lever, feeling her head start to buzz as the air expanded in her chest. Blowing out a few bubbles to ease the pressure, she tried to ignore the burning sensation and went on pressing, pressing. The lever loosened in her hands and she knew that she could do no more. The pain in her head and chest overcame her. She sank to the bottom.

Hands thumped painfully on her back and from a great distance away someone was calling her name urgently. Must be an emergency call, she thought vaguely, then coughed and spluttered as she tried to speak. The hands wouldn't leave her alone, they kept pummelling her and rubbing her vigorously until she could stand it no longer. 'All right, all right, I'm coming,' she managed.

Something that sounded like a relieved laugh came from above her and she turned to find Bruce kneeling over her. She tried to sit up, but he wouldn't let her. There was a curiously guarded expression in his eyes.

'Why didn't you leave me to drown, Felicity? It would have been a perfect revenge for you, wouldn't it? My life for your brother's?'

Felicity stared at him, unable to speak.

'Answer me! Why didn't you let me drown?'

'I—I couldn't let you die.'

'But why risk your life trying to save mine?'

'Because I . . .' She stopped abruptly.

'Say it, Felicity, say it!'

'Because I love you. I love you so much, it hurts. Is that what you wanted to hear?' she said bitterly, tears mingling with the sea-water on her face.

She had spoken in little more than a whisper, but Bruce had heard her quite clearly. He gave a little sigh, as if he had just arrived home after a long journey. He let her sit up and she looked round blindly for her beach wrap.

'What about your promise to your mother?'

For a moment she was still, then said steadily, 'My mother's dead. She died over a week ago.' Standing up, she turned to face him. 'I received a letter from a relative this morning. You were right about my brother all along. He did everything you said he did and more besides. It seems it runs in the family, like you said,' she added with bitter

187

self-contempt. 'I know it's inadequate and you won't care anyway, but I just wanted to say that I'm sorry for what I did to you.' She turned away, unable to meet the look of derision that she knew would be in his eyes after her pathetic confession.

Bruce didn't try to stop her, but he said her name softly. She halted but kept her back towards him.

'Have I ever lied to you, Felicity?' he said unexpectedly.

'N-no.'

'Then you must believe this.' Taking her gently in his arms, he turned her round to face him. His lips touched her neck, explored the line of her cheek and then sought her mouth. His kiss was warm, loving, but soon became as demanding as it had been during the hurricane, and Felicity found herself responding without reserve, abandoning herself to the need within her. At last they drew apart and she stared at him, tears of happiness in her eyes.

'You still love me,' she said joyfully, incredulously. 'But I thought you hated me.'

He held her close in his arms, unable to let her go. 'No, never that! I admit that for a time I wanted to hurt you as much as you had hurt me, but I never stopped loving you and I was sure that you loved me in return, but it was hell waiting for you to realise how you really felt about me. That's why I gave you the three-year ultimatum. I had to keep you here, and I thought that even you would recognise your true feelings by then.'

'I didn't until I got the cablegram from England and knew that I didn't want to leave you, ever, even if you did treat me like dirt for the rest of my life.'

'I know.'

'You did? But how?'

He hesitated, then smiled ruefully. 'The Postmaster phoned me to apologise for the delay with your cable. After a few casual questions I gleaned the contents. I thought you'd got someone to send it to you, so I came home early in case you decided to bolt. I waited all evening for you to say something; then I saw you throwing the flowers in the sea and realised it was true. I'm sorry about your mother, Felicity.'

Burying her head in his shoulder and finding great comfort thereby, she said quietly, 'She was eaten up by her own bitterness. I couldn't see that when I was with her, but I can now. She never knew I'd married you. I'm glad she didn't know.'

Quickly he changed the subject. 'Why didn't you tell me why you were going to Jamaica today? Just before I came out to find you I had an irate telephone call from a charter pilot still waiting for you in Kingston. He also told me about Geoff's marriage.'

'I knew you wouldn't believe me. And besides, I wasn't altogether sure you'd approve about Edwina and Geoff.'

'On the contrary, I'm delighted. One less predatory male for me to worry about in the vicinity of my wonderful wife!'

Felicity looked at him mistily. 'Oh, I don't deserve that.'

'You deserve everything you're going to get, with this to start with.' Almost roughly, he pulled her into his arms again, his mouth finding hers with passionate intensity, a fierce hunger in his lips that would take no refusal, making the world spin round her head until she could think of nothing but the need to respond to his embrace. When at last he put her from him she was quivering with awareness. 'You'd better go and change. Put on a pretty dress,' he said thickly.

'Are we going out?' she asked with some disappointment. 'Where?'

'You'll see. Go on, before I give way to temptation.'

Placing her hands on his smooth, bare chest, she said softly, 'Bruce, I—I wouldn't mind if we stayed home this evening.'

He muttered something under his breath and then scooped her up in his arms and carried her towards the

189

house. 'I know, little one, but first there's something we must do.'

The car ride was different from any they had ever taken before; whenever he safely could, Bruce took his hand from the wheel and covered hers, his eyes bright and triumphant. They circuited the brilliantly lit town where the noise of the steel bands still echoed dimly, and drew up beside the little stone church on the hillside.

'I thought we should ask for a blessing on our marriage,' Bruce said simply, and took her hand as they walked up the steps.

Felicity paused in the doorway and looked out over the island she had come to love. That, and the man beside her who had led her safely out of darkness into happiness. The moment for which she had waited so long had come at last.

YOU'LL L♥VE
Harlequin Magazine

for women who enjoy reading fascinating stories of exciting romance in exotic places

SUBSCRIBE NOW!

This is a colorful magazine especially designed and published for the readers of Harlequin novels.

Now you can receive your very own copy delivered right to your home every month throughout the year for only 75¢ an issue.

This colorful magazine is available only through Harlequin Reader Service, so enter your subscription now!

In every issue...

Here's what you'll find:

♥ a complete, full-length romantic novel...illustrated in color.

♥ exotic travel feature...an adventurous visit to a romantic faraway corner of the world.

♥ delightful recipes from around the world...to bring delectable new ideas to your table.

♥ reader's page...your chance to exchange news and views with other Harlequin readers.

♥ other features on a wide variety of interesting subjects.

Start enjoying your own copies of Harlequin magazine immediately by completing the subscription reservation form.

Not sold in stores!